LUCY CHURCH
AMIABLY

FIRST U.S. EDITION

GERTRUDE STEIN

A Novel of Romantic beauty and nature and
which Looks Like an Engraving

LUCY CHURCH
AMIABLY

*And with a nod she turned her head
toward the falling water. Amiably.*

NEW YORK

Something Else Press, Inc.

238 WEST 22nd STREET

1969

L. C. Catalog Card No: 78-82530

Originally published in 1930. Reissued, 1969, by Something Else Press, Inc., 238 West 22nd Street, New York, N.Y. 10011.

Manufactured in the United States of America

ADVERTISEMENT

Lucy Church Amiably. There is a church and it is in Lucey and it has a steeple and the steeple is a pagoda and there is no reason for it and it looks like something else. Beside this there is amiably and this comes from the paragraph.

Select your song she said and it was done and then she said and it was done with a nod and then she bent her head in the direction of the falling water. Amiably.

This altogether makes a return to romantic nature that is it makes a landscape look like an engraving in which there are some people, after all if they are to be seen there they feel as pretty as they look and this makes it have a river a gorge an inundation and a remarkable meadowed mass which is whatever they use not to feed but to bed cows. Lucy Church Amiably is a novel of romantic beauty and nature and of Lucy Church and John Mary and Simon Therese.

271274

BEGINS THE MIDDLE OF MAY
INTRODUCTION

There were as many chairs there and there were two a chair that can be found everywhere a rocking chair that is to say a rocking chair can be found everywhere. Two there one at one end and the other at the other end. They were in front of the building and in sitting and rocking there was a very slight declivity in front of the building.

The husband had been in England. The wife had been brought up by a family that had had her mother there and this gave such a gracious pair an additional restoration of their share. Having a daughter she had married a man who because of wounds or because of character made it inevitable that she should falter and so having left it more than a mother two children for this and that brought to her.

No history of a family to close with those and close. Never shall he be alone to be alone to be alone to be alone to them to lend a hand and leave it left and wasted. Having bowed her to a seat.

A genius says that when he is not successful he is

treated with consideration like a genius but when he is successful and has been as rich as successful he is treated like anybody by his family. For this reason he does not believe that a family is necessary necessarily a family and a family is a mother and a brother and a sister and a sister and a nephew and nieces and a brother-in-law who is a doctor. This is what makes genius conversational the very best thing that has and can happen so it is said to be a gift which is like fish and bread and butter very well served after a considerable delay. How often are they where they were anxious to go oftener and later and letting it be left to them. Be raised by a mother and taught by a father who is not known as another and many choose different branches of a specialty. What were his feelings when he had awakened. That he had lost a picture. And he had. It had happened on that trip and on that day. And his conscience did not declare him to have been equally pleasant when he refused his nephew the opportunity for a change of residence that his nephew desired. To let it be considered as displacing not only rivers but water lakes and electricity. He could never interest himself in such a question.

Mr. and Mrs. Paul Daniel went to a part of the country which when it was in apparent order was not only acceptable but convenient they hoped there to find a house which would be suited to them and there not considered familiarly it would be best not to have them visiting. Not at all as rubbish. It is

very well known that earlier those who were not satisfied with best left alone were accustomed to be let alone. There has been more nearly sensitiveness equally distributed than either she or they admit. Admittedly.

There can be no inheritance of the jewels as well as the case even if both have been and are to be sold. And replaced by bronze of which there is no particular concerning which there is no particular oratory. Roses open.

There are very often in the middle of May many ways of going to and leaving the country. There are a great many people missing and missed who would very much have wished to be seen then. And after a while it made be very often what was apparently as they wished. This is why very often a worker in enamels marries a country doctor's daughter and vice versa.

A little after one and two they arrived. They were in time for their meal because there is no more preparation needed when agriculture assumes that importance. Let it believe that it is for the best that if there are four children the youngest one should be a girl.

A family might be a prize.

Holmer Arthur Elmer and Barber all wear aprons and usually they are lost as to a chalice and with it a chance to be used in succession as if as they wish. This makes a family more particularly on sufferance.

He said if you were said to be dead and dead cer-

tain that it was marketable would it be marketable Tuesday. The middle of May is in that state.

White and delight.

He had three illegitimate children and he had been frequently married as well.

He had been as well known as when he had seen them come from a distance. After every little while he endeavoured to engage them in their having thought it very well to be mentioned.

In this when is it if there are very many in every way and one of them one out of five leaves for two weeks and is not replaced and hitherto there had been six it was very frequently necessary that there is interference. Counting them as dahlias.

In a little more of it which is by train by aeroplane or by accidentally witnessing rain in a little more of it it is not desirable that as there is no difference it is just as well that very many are mentioned. She would like to speak.

Imagining that it would be that he having her she not having other than they they being left in and about and if he were useful usefully could it be that the only desirability would be returned as if not having left for eighteen months while they were leaving it as if in some to taste winter is as might it be enjoyed. All gold is put into water and all water is put into butter and all butter is put into apples and all apples are put into trees and all trees are put into flourishing and all flourishing is put into welcome and all welcome is put into translation and all translation is resisting

to their having felt that it was most and best and
called called it at the time that it was actually reunited
in spite of their addition of which and whether it is
mine. He made many many tickle them as well as
well as withstand.

A professional interest in liking made easy easy
easier.

In this way introduced to left left left right left.

If wean weaned and Nanette spoke she very in a
very in a very in a very very very pointed and excep-
tional with stood. The daughter was simple minded.

There is no reason why why why why why why
two two troubled in there and man.

In this story there is to be not only white black
tea colour and vestiges of their bankruptcy but also
well wishing and outlined and melodious and with a
will and much of it to be sure with their only arrangement certainly for this for the time of which when
by the way what is the difference between fixed.

Lucy is well able to undertake the care of it presently. Paul wishes his name spelt as it has been.
William planned a wedding surreptitiously and Mary
was if one might say so very nearly as she stood. Historically weeding makes it be that they are modified
by their love and delight. Historically received
Louis for Edward. It is very little known that they
are right.

It is the answer any of their being more often
much more than it could. He had been at a gather-

ing and wished it to be a replica and very well then. This is the day to obey. Obedient.

Arthur John Carnagan matched silk. He began in reality to be planned enigmatically and with the best reiteration which is by this as they leave it out. There can be everywhere three with care. Here we have five. This historically here we have five. One whole and in part left to school school it. Second whole and in part easily and left it all here all here. Next and left left to be shoved away and more more having his be at a distant distance and then one. One such an overwhelming instance of reciprocity. This is to be a history of the five as alive does it makc any difference who said who said and suppose suppose and arose and very well six the one who being often made to go to shoes made finally a leading grain to grain. Six then with a weeding and as no objection can be made as much as they like liked let us easily endow Samson. Sit easily and well one on a horse one on a door one on a shore one on a crest one on a kindled sale and one also made crowning this in sight. It is very well known will then.

CHAPTER II

To wish to remember that every year is a change if it is to be considered historically.

Every year is a change if it is to be considered historically.

Six characters all of them having brothers. A novel called the Two Brothers is very well named.

There can be in the way of making a distance be ten when it is ten when it is very passably sixty and sixteen all of it considered whether it is better to be left by the time that after all busily not to go there.

Lamartine is not a queen.

Brillat-Savarin is not endowed with one being elder.

Claudel is a mountain which is is is a cascade which is is is a little better than where bread actually and white of egg actually is reputed.

Paulet may be the name of their villainy he was never not only privately an advantage in inquiring were they at home but also vindicated by resisting inadmissably which caused very nearly by himself because it was the cause of his arrest. Arrested.

Furthermore there is placed further there is placed to place one who not only causes but because he is the cause of there being no one here and there on the fourth and on the fourteenth of July. Imagine no one is here here and there on the fourth and on the fourth and fourteenth of July.

Believing that a woman who is not only not in an instance of being very well and readily adaptable remember Madame Recamier died in poverty.

In every instance there is a difference between history and geography.

Let it make a cause to celebrate if to be at once is to state that they are fleeting.

It happened that after six weeks and accidentally a distant mountain was seen. It is very possible to mistake snow for sun and is for whether it is or is not an advantage. Tobacco can be grown also in the place of a fear that it may be too late various things. This is the type of landscape which when having been in communication with those who wish who wish to be left in land in land and liking it at most with running with running water in land with running water and very like very likely very liked and with it as it was to be had with no more hesitation than in a meadow. The great question does delicate mean backward and does Felicite need society in other words words and details of which and when it is possible to remove trees not in the sense of becoming but of replanting.

And rejoice.

Connect and connected. It is very agreeable that it is what is not only hazardous but at one time their choice their choosing their substituting their whether it shows more or less variety to have it stem it in time a stitch in time saves nine.

Once every once in a while not religiously but regularly they fastened the curtain back. In many cases there has never been a time when there was as much indulgence shown for length and leaving. In a little while planted and transplanted made it endure and as durable as with this with this with the door.

A priest can deplore that in a little more than doubtfully relieved it should be not more useful than is readily left to them to those who mean to fasten parts of it in the desirable desirability of their liking.

Pleasing it to be carefully left to them.

Now knowing very well just what it looks like perhaps anybody can be parried.

In between, thirteen, twenty-three, three, thirty and a million or three. How many parts of metal make men women and in this country never children adequate to the duty which produces very much as much as is needed. They need what they have.

If everybody does date arising with rising and much as if it were with very well when do nettles do nettles do nettles do do do feed. They do ducks and fowls as well as fed cooked with and in plenty and a pleasure as well as an occupation. Once more very much as if it had been very well nourished and at all and in and a pledge a pledge of when then.

18

If every one can if there has been attention be be bought be bought taught are they well well to do do and date it as if nearly all of it as freight and bait. A very tall and successful horticulture.

This is the money around and the day around and the evening around and the lay of the land.

He went away and he questioned them partly.

Did a little thing make a difference.

Were they worried by sheep.

Do orange coloured mushrooms grow in thickets and were they mother and daughter or only neighbours.

He asked one at a time.

How many halves have been arranged as magnolias.

He made it be as if he had called up from below Will you give me the keys. And what was he answered. Why yes certainly if you will wait a minute.

He might be very well liked half of the time and because of this he was very much more than pleasant as it is very well known that at all times there is a day and a half which is dedicated to agriculture in the sense of gardening as a necessity in times of extreme distress that is after and before.

He was individually left in no doubt that this is when and where they were to be day in and day out day in and day out.

Leaving it as in the most and after all their best they gave their best attention to it.

Generally generally as it is as much as they will be very capable of leaving it higher that is when snow

mountains are covered anteriorly with sun and separate bases of leaving below not a meadow not a prairie but a straight surface as an attraction which is called a bottom when once there is water when once there is water. We who do.

How can novels be as close as close closing not being not being bent but to open openly shown that they have been have been in in invariable and plain explain the variety of plentiful interpellation of theirs two and two.

What was it that she was adding as she was standing and leaving. They are later and earlier in that way that way and organisation.

If men say women and women say women who is to know paper from paper. She said suddenly withstand and she said with and with widen and she said they have been added as lingering with it having satisfied left to right which means that that can acutely be an accidental precaution.

She said. Who made it do.

Select your song she said and it was done and then she said and it was done with a nod and then she bent her head in the direction of the falling water. Amiably.

To leave on the thirtieth and to arrive on the second and to be on the way on the fourth and to be settled by the fourteenth and to be having word of their decision on the sixteenth and to be forgiven on the seventeenth not twice but once. This makes it as noiseless as ever.

She said. It is a great pleasure to put it there.

She said it is a great pleasure when it is there. She said. It is not only necessary but needful and for many reasons and because of not having any present plan. She said that it was not very well said.

There is no difference between safety and century.

What happened when they were weaned. They happened to have been betrothed and being careful. Also they met their very prettily met their very much as if they met with it there where any little added is not only seen but probably meant to be with them. Insomuch in between is what mountains are.

And Lamartine.

How old are they when they are they to sit at the table and eat.

There are three ways of going and coming.

There are four ways of preparing and receiving.

There are five ways of hearing of it.

There is it is not of any use or purpose to deny that they might might be conversing about how it comes and why it is not only very much but very much of it. Let it be with a stream.

Every time Claudel wrote he spoke and vice versa.

When there is no liking or even love of fragrant flowers and the barely well known is at the time which is very nearly a dislike for them. Not nearly a dislike for them to feel and to abide by.

They came to say happily it happened to-day and not some other day. How can it be possible that by the time they were there they could be of no assistance.

While a while.

She and he both were sitting by the side of a running brook and they were not troubled by the noise on the whole they found it agreeable.

Miche is not Michel. It is ed i belle. This is all well. Says my very famous Belle not Belley. This is to introduce Lamartine to a queen. This is to introduce Lamartine and seen. This is to introduce Claudel as well. This is to introduce Severine in between. Severine and Savarin when they came and when they ran they do not run when they can walk so quickly with their life as it is very well known.

Supposing every one lived at one time what would they say. They would observe that stringing string beans is universal.

Living at one time does not make two at one time. Living at one time does not make one at one time. Feeding nettles to ducks and chickens does not make graduation and raspberries and strawberries in autumn do not change Bertha to Barbara to Belle to William Tell.

Arouse aloud is what they say when they have been living in every way. What could it eat if it were edible.

A great many who went away came back but not to the same place because having been used to yellow shoes made of yellow leather they prefer to go and come altogether. This was the same to them.

How very difficult is it for Aunt Fanny to be sad but it has been done and is and why not because of the return or order but because of the difference.

Supposing they are very rich then there needs watchfulness, but supposing they are not very rich supposing that they are rich but not richer then it does not need watchfulness it does not need watchfulness it does not need watchfulness.

How many throw what they use to do with it. This is the boy who was not afraid and yet when he was escaping they said be careful of the salad that is there.

A little bit of taste of hay and this is this is what they say the hay and wheat and grass and peas and will it will it at their ease he came from here and the first thing he did was to go to a large house.

In a large house he found that they were at home and so forth.

There is a difference in defence of John Mary Tudor and the rest. He went away gradually having had gradually fishes and the birds gradually he went away and there it was that it behove him to leave a little apple rabbit there and singing and by very much of it as in mischance he to be elaborated could and sell at once by this with not a wedding inclined further. It was rarely that there was so much activity engendered as by his so after the bequest. Bequest and whom. He was killed at noon.

Some say some say two away two away two away three a day at and play let it be theirs not to know where at the seaside it will be such a pleasure for them to go.

It is very easy for it to be profitable.

When do they love to get richer melodiously with dandelion and in precision. It is very well to be richer and tell and tell it in such a way that they join hands. He said he said not that he said universally and university in very much what what is a foxglove.

Naturally there is in every once in a while a century and there is in every once in a while a century when they are rich of course rich of course when they are rich of course.

When they are rich of course.

To thank think quickly.

Every time that they to thank think quickly rich of course making it as a very well when it is that it is with a very nearly as it is just as a cherished in the ribbon. Who can count ribbons if they are told that it is very likely why there are elephants.

Can it be told symmetrically that very many ruins are with a sound as sound as a sound tobacco oil from nuts hay from corn sleeping from their distance which yesterday was water and to-day and what is it when wealth is with a vim.

Letting centuries have privately owned baths.

Letting everybody be rich. Everybody is rich and what is a dandelion dandelion dandelion dandelion, what is a dandelion with or without hers.

If everybody is rich two and two make four one and one make two two and two and two.

There is no difference between younger and older between told and told her between him and between

him. There is no difference hurriedly. When this is said said said said.

Very well up there so yes very well up there.

This is the way of it as they as they this is the way of said and say they are rich and richer every day in the ordinary meaning of the word.

This letting it be seen telling welling that it is to be seen tell well that it is to be seen that every one being well to do well to do how do you do.

Everybody who is through.

Through with it.

Lamentably.

Everybody who is through through with it lamentably.

To suppose wind is from the direction from which it comes, this makes the formation of the clouds very much as much as if they were there in inches.

Beside this if the desire to go on in a day makes it as if to say never to say so in their behalf.

There is no inexactitude in riches and richer.

How can it be that a drama which they see has to be has to be indifferently that if as ever they are more than that behind.

There is no difference at all whether it is he or having him or his or held or Brillat Savarin or their laudation or by the time or with a window and respect or in respect to losses losses of wild pansies which can be used as an infusion none of these make any difference permanently as they are all rich.

Excused as do as date and dates and prepared plenty advantageously. An original placing it up and down theirs and hindrance. And how many times have they been betrothed.

No difference between as rich and talking.

Let it be every one as rich as rich as rich as letting it be every one as rich as rich as rich and letting it be letting it be every one as rich.

There may be worry but there can not be poverty there can be worry but there cannot be poverty there can be worry there can be worry there can be worry but there can not be poverty.

Everybody sits alone and not everybody sits alone and not and everybody sits alone and not everybody sits alone.

Nobody sits alone who is not here and here and everybody who sits alone is everybody who is here and here. Everybody anybody.

There is no redress for baby could not help it now. Now or endow. Endow Yenne. Why. Because everybody finds their cake delicious.

Coming back.

Who lived here.

What are the persons who have had a house.

Was it by the time that it was an advantage that they planted poplars.

In time for this in particular and practically by the best way of passing within an appreciable distance of it.

Nobody can know why he was very willing to be serviceable.

In case and out out and out and going with a and without a father and son.

It is currently expected that very many follow with another.

In this and sweetly.

Having been very likely that the bell rang.

CHAPTER III

They marry.

If she made it easy to read the marriage contract a contract to marry. If she made it easy for the imitation and the other one who could call following false cock false cock and no answer. And by the best of embroidery which is white with a delicate touch. And so they marry marry marry three.

When this you see you can marry me. When this you see you can marry me marry marry undeniably marry and see see that orchids are brown and withal withal withal intent.

It is undeniably an undeniably undertaken intentionally when this you see and marry me and precisely in established inter marriage with coming to be to be integrally undeniably.

Having settled that every one is rich and richer how many have they in it. To begin to mean Lamartine and Bonnat. Bonnat has been called Bennett and as such was torn away from the salad and the result of a courageous boy with a cart a boy being a young man and stirred. By and by he was ahead and

not behead beheaded. Please be in difference indifference by their pleasure.

There are there separate stories and stones and five.

He was a student in a College where he learned to love and long and afterwards as there were no clouds and even riches and very much just observation of the causes of their celebration so much so that curtains are supper and surprises there would be conversation and hear them speak.

Speak urgently.

A great many and right and rights and rights and right right right a religious rite. That is especially in conversation. That is one effective underlying withal and arise arising by daylight.

Conversation can be seen.

When all the same they are rich and two try tries trimestre and tried. Tiring makes finally forget me nots easily. And so to seen. Two seen and or and oriole and an edible bird.

Mistakenly.

If everybody is rich when are mountains covered with snow. We know.

Some say that everything away means eating at noon.

This does change daughters to mothers.

Bonnat was killed not by the regular attackers but by the aid of a boy who was a young man and pushed a cart as a cover.

Conversation about character.

It is very rare to see three brothers working together and if there is an exodus there will not be more than old and young and young and old. And in between when medallions of letting it alone are strung. In this way they are different in their turn to apples grapes cakes and further destruction of three trees which are valuable only in so far as there are stretches of wood and listening.

Make birds be birds and poppies be poppies and astonomers be astronomers.

This is the third supposition. When this you see remember to see Lamartine Claudel Bonnat and Severine and more having more having and more having more having a very little longer and shorter.

Conversation whether standing or sitting.

Everybody is rich quietly. Everybody is as rich quietly.

Do do do edible birds fly and make a little noise very nearly as if they had their wings held closely and resemble what is like them there.

Do edible birds fly in the air and hold their wings close as close as if they were as much as they were when they were there. Edible birds in the air flying from there and to there. Edible birds as edible birds in the air flying with wings as closely as they are there.

This is why three one four and no more. Three sons and a girl a mother and a father a grandmother and a grandfather and a simple-minded daughter and

as conversation green string beans and in order in order to make it change more more and more.

Very and left left and very very and very very left and very. How many are there in there with this and a drawing very well. A drawing very well and fifty thousand.

Felicite can be in with a pasturage as well. Would it would it if it would it.

Nobody knows how cars can close and laden be the in the main. Is there more exercise in in and out. How very beautifully the air makes its passage from here to there.

Sometimes there are four or five and sometimes, there are five or six.

Five or six in a fix four or five all after all.

How can they be impatient with use it.

There is no difference between at a distance and why will they till it.

Until it is not a temptation. Until it is not a temptation until it is not a temptation.

Very nearly have a hare.

And to think of it differently.

It did does have to be to smell like box which is a plant and odouriferous.

John Mary Bonnat made a face of pleasurable enjoyment when he was not admitted and allowed in place of cultivation to prepare escapes. Two escapes and to be hindered. If he had wished to wash an automobile in the morning he would have had plenty of time if it had not been for the inconvenience that

if there has been a lack of rain there will not be an abundance of flow of water in the evening.

This leading to that as conferring plentifully what each one did.

In or out.

It is very difficult to be interested as you know.

If he was right would it be that she had feared that there would not be many more apples as they see apple apple with it.

The life and times of any of them who have eaten what has been mentioned. What has been mentioned. Mr. Claudel has not only been here but being very well known has bought a house this is not because of the departure of a dear friend but because as many do he finds it a pleasant place to live in too.

Mr. Brillat Savarin was installed here and after all what does it matter if they always look down or they come up not from a plateau but from a plain. A plain in very distant if one comes across it. Bonnat is notorious as having been dead dead did it. Lamartine is not nearly as nearly as if every wind blew clouds away. This makes fifty-seven fairly appetising as if Therese had a mother Fred a father and Germaine a sister. Does any of that make sizes separately laid carefully here and there when very nearly every baker has a handsome son. There is very little character in omnipresent. How many houses are there in it. It does not make a particle of difference if it is intermittent not a particle.

If it is true that they came and went why should thirty be thirty-three.

Recollection as well as well never see the sea.

It is not as they come that they are here.

He said busily just the same and he said stop not stop it. He said stop.

He said ways and means of backwards and forwards.

He said religion and going up and down if it comes to mountains and there is a road how many precipices are there on it. None at all.

He said men and women make children and children do have by and by the cooking which is very sweet and naturally an insult if at last. This makes went to pieces.

Do do very well have it around the eyes. Not if with having been Marius or left to please her.

He said he was Claudel.

She said very well.

He said he was Brillat Savarin. He said he was Lamartine. He said he was Bonnat. Not at the same time not in the same place. There is no difference between from here to here and there is no difference between statues and must. Who can see the beauty of poplar trees. Who can see the beauty of poplar trees. Not to be rough with them who can see the beauty of poplar trees. Who can see the beauty of poplar trees.

What is it.

Having seen candles in a theater.

What is it.

What is it.

Having seen borders in colour.

What is it.

What is it.

What is the colour of butter and peculiar violence of nuts if nuts are made into oil and oil is ineradicable.

She moved very silently making a noise.

Toys noise and very quietly as if there was land in Asia.

Who makes it be after this yes and a drop a drop from that height there.

Overflow avalanche in union there is strength in the meantime declared it is what is a most additional poise.

This is the art of conversation which is lessened by their intention and with a willing have they the habit of their leaning.

Mr. and Mrs. Paul William which is a cause of their perturbation. They removed from a closed window to an open one but she did not think so. It is very useful to be allowed three one cold one warm and one heated. It is very useful to be allowed one cold one warm one heated. It is very useful to be as they wish. It. Might it be the occasion of his tiring. Lessons in economy. To let it be careful and a provision. To let it be a provision. Might he be careful and not let it be a provision. Might he be careful and not let it be a provision. Particularly withstood.

If to see the tree if to see very well I thank you.

Mr. Marin Mr. Hulbard Mr. Dartmouth and Mr. Henry have all of them named trees trees. Very well I thank you.

Mr. Arthur Mr. Hayes Mr. William have all named meadows and trees meadows meadows and trees indecision. All three have attempted to allow distant snow to show that is pleasantly all land. All three have been very much influenced by little knolls inclosing a stone. They also have been failing in changing planting for plantation. There can be corn tobacco grain and beet crops if they wish for winter. How many poplar trees are there on it and how large do they grow in thirty-five years ordinarily. As even as they wish to be surrounded by knolls which have been made by reason of there being there.

To wish to smell thyme mint and various very odouriferous low growing and easily drying herbage.

This is what makes them tempt them to go away.

Well and whether more than ever.

If she had three boys and they were very well adapted to that how much would there be doubt of how they felt. Negro hair can felt that is to say can be felted that is to say can be felt and because of this made partly and set apart. Every time that he is willing to have been received let it alone. What is the difference what they are like.

A novel instance of what is the difference what they are like.

Let it be louder than allowed and let it be what is

addressing an animal. If you do it again I will turn
my back and by this I will mean that I find it intoler-
able not really but additionally and very well wait.
You can very well wait.

Hinting at climax. To change weather and short-
age and pink and green herbage and glass and industry
and violets and not at once. Any made of metal is
clear. Retire to axes and oxen to ashes and to
widows and to windows and to very suddenly. What
is the difference what has been purchased. It is in
this way that they are on the ground where after
which and when they like to have left not that which
is made in duplicate and duplicated. Let us go slowly. To commence then.

There is no doubt that they are stout just as they
have been thin.

That is many at a time with there.

Make it be a wife slowly. She was not sad specif-
ically with their pleasure that it was mostly as if they
were called. Is there any difference if you see it or
if you leave it. There is no difference between laying
it down and with it all as if they had parcelled it out
to them and they had some use for it. Would they
go on if they were not spoken to. There is an answer.
Let it be that they are interested in their stairs. There
are no stairs where there is no up and down. Who
made whose be very willing all the same. Atchison
Topeka and Santa Fé when this is not the month of
May.

Back again to pattie hot and as many craw fish

as can be seen to be cold. And then they were very careful to have bands together and something that is a flower and is known as a Roman candle. These things are interesting and peculiar and every once every may they may see a mountain which has snow after all in what is everybody interested. In what they see. When this you see remember me.

To see scenery and to be adaptable and to like what is had and to be murmuring this is very well thought of here and to refuse to be left to them. No interest in why they like butter. The time has now come to interst them favouring their best way of asking why have they been winning and if they have been winning let it be a lesson to them to gather together altogether. Everybody knows my name.

When after all it was part of the time and there can be a dislike of many skies which have sky-larks which are not singing at dark but in the country which is open and very often looking attentively at hearing many many have a million or three eventually as an eventuality. Please listen to this it is very interesting. Nobody knows which name is the one they have heard. Very well I thank you. Nobody knows how very pleasantly butter burns. Nobody. Nobody can be in doubt of undertaking their dispatch. Nobody. Nobody has been very careful of a sofa which is to be left in her care and she is very careful of a sofa which has been left in her care. This is the beginning and if this is the beginning this is the beginning of dissatisfaction with men and women and child-

ren and so forth and does it matter which is pleas-
anter a snow mountain or a river or a tree which is a
poplar.

Oh yes she says oh yes and when she says oh yes
she says oh yes oh yes she says oh yes.

It is best to be there. There are very many different ways of leading left to it and more than at once
with them as they feel it being with this as if under
the influence of quiet and very well met with a mayor
of this very well known and as interesting part of this
very admittedly advantageous country.

Nicely if it is not too much to undertake to undergo
because there has been more than one occasion. There
have been two brigands. One in eighteen hundred
and four and one in eighteen hundred and forty-four
and one in eighteen ninety seven.

The brigand in eighteen hundred and four was mistaken for another nationality once when he was travelling. The one in eighteen hundred and forty four died
after he had been noticed as withdrawing from their
observation. The one in eighteen ninety-seven is the
one who was not daring when he entered and found
out nothing but later on he withstood everything and
later on he was attacked and he succumbed when there
was some one who was not from the time that he could
see he could see the time as he was known to be at
morning and evening in the morning. The police
were aided by a man and he was therefor not only not
bewildered but finally actively destroyed as is in perfectly conversing. Why should they be as much as

they have in vegetable gardening. Answer me that.

There is no difference between account and accounting and recount and recounting.

Why does it have theirs stirring. A novel in time. Time as you very well know makes mountains. Time as you very well know makes it be that chairs go with sofas and pleasures with foot-stools. Time as you very well know make it not different to understand spoken at a distance if they have an acute hearing and pleasure is for prediction. Time as you may or may not know is known to be left and right. Time as you may know may be very well there. Very well I thank you. It is a settlement of inevitably a piece of beginning means very well I thank you as it makes a sequal. There are three sequals excellently. Leave let it be welcome to their home. If she had been going on she would have met him. If they have it be in voices voices of which they are often proud to make it tell that which is as if they had once said in a flood candles in a flood and also she is very foolish to be women with as if a flood a flooding extra and also candle sticks. So there was. That makes three. When this you see remember me to them. Now they must be as well as they must be as well as at a time when very little leaves out. There is no difference between fathers daughters sons sisters brothers mothers and their images. Any little way all to. All to go. All to go to come where. Where is there a left to right. Where is there but it is. Where is there will or welling where is there asking if it is accept-

able. Acceptably. May we imagine that a bow is
usual. Very well I thank you.

Three times across once with a loss four times with
a sentry three times with their best effort and once
or twice restlessly and three or four times individually
and five times one at a time and so forth. The warmth
can rise. Everybody who tries it does not succeed.

Five and five over five. Five fifty five. Fifty
five and fifty over forty forty five. It is very usual
to think of a name. Follow me after follow me after
follow me after follow me.

It would really be important.

If something looks like that it is that and so a
beginning of a settlement is made by Madame Munet
of Artemarre and this is not an invention as all the
rest is all the rest is this is not an invention as all the
rest is as all the rest is.

Having seen every one as they were every one
was there. And once more it is noticeable that heat
can arise from the ground with varying conditions
of wind and moisture and methods of wishing chestnut trees to bear their nuts so that they would not
be an obligation to a festival. They welcome them
all.

Boughs and walking in front of his horse as if a
horse and a wagon were not there the wagon being
very well adapted to riding. Is there any distance
between a horse a buggy and a man. Very well I
thank you. It is meant that they did not change
lightening for flooding and flooding for ringing and

ringing for honey-suckle and as yet. As yet it was
very carefully planned.

Might they be an obstacle to further progress as
well as a description of a man who has been willing
to be chosen as one of four.

On account of it. Many many are a hundred and
twenty. And a hundred and twenty after twenty
five are two hundred and twenty. And two hundred
and twenty after twenty six and two hundred and
twenty are two hundred and thirty and after two
hundred thirty they will be especially favoured. This
is why there are the remainder and the remainder
which is four times four or sixty four is a remainder
that is thought of as having been left to themselves
exactly. Be left to right with it as in a way. In a
way she has been told that when they were there it
was naturally naturally an instance of advantage.

Concentrated meat and crackers not when they
were known not where they were known not where
they were known not when they were known. It is
very difficult for thunder to make a noise which is
why they are coming to have it seen as a preference.
Preferred. Let lambs have it just the same. All
this makes towels with a lisp and letting white be said.
White be said beside.

Boughs and willing to see.

Boughs and willing to say.

Boughs and willing to say so and willing to say so.

Boughs and willing willing to say willing to say

willing to say so.   Prepared.   It is best never to have
it prepared just prepared justly prepared.

Coming now to believe relief.

He was relieved.

She was relieved.

She was relieved to be here.

He was relieved to be here.

He was relieved to be here.

It is very doubtful if there is any difference between hail and rain between between hail and rain.

It is very doubtful if there is any relation between
at last and at least.   It is very doubful if there is any
difference between at last and at least.   It is very
doubtful if there is any difference between at least
between at last between at last between at least.   It
is very doubtful if there is any difference between at
last and at least.

CHAPTER IV

If one who had been named Bonnard is dead what is god given god given what is god given with a simple civilian. This is Tuesday. Tuesday is coloured by M. Claudel having been thought to be left to them largely left to them largely left to them largely Mr. Lamartine which is why Ernest is busily happily and also and because also pine trees with a little flag on top greet regiments and also because if it wills if it wills to remain a swallow a very significant swallow not to study a place of in place of intrusion and also prepare a church to be not only for houses horses wagons pushed and also automobiles and they have frequently to use it as their home below on top. Action and actions. How many knives can Lucy clean with a machine. The life of Josephine. If she is asked to come back and she is she will afterwards be very far from having been placed where she was where she was where she was. Hours and hours where she was. At first it was very quiet afterwards it was just as quiet it remained just as quiet. At first it was just as quiet it was just as quiet afterwards it was just as quiet.

There are four kinds of left to right.

Left to right with remaining differently. Left and right with restfulness restfulness of their being identically withstood as if there was a difficulty of backward and forward. Left and right without any doubt of which hesitation takes more space than a little in an animated compliment of which it was repeated. Left and right in recalling their having been why they were wishing for this if you please.

A name and negroes have neither better nor more loves. To be more finally withstood withstood withstood still stilled withstood with still still as well as why there are women. Women women women girls girls girls girls girls girls how many houses have been asked will you come again. Now then. There is no difference between left and right may we be willing to see about it.

There is politenes if if if they they they are are are are not what they were. We too we too are left to learning where it is very difficult to arrange for when there is more than there is blue in gold and rose in gold and will it be a pleasure to have them be fairly unitedly one two three.

Nobody is out when it is raining nobody is out when it is raining unless they have been prepared to be much more aware of that than they are they were.

It is of no interest that the largest tree in the wood is measured from left to right left to right right to left with more of them above than below. There is really no question about how they do not sing.

Open open open roses.

It came when it it came it came to many more than sweetness sweetness of fruit and this is when there is no in and out in and out and around around and will and shall shall and made of it practically as an inference.

What will it be will it be.

It is easier to listen than to look. To be as and can.

It is safely with a welcome welcome and they cannot go. They cannot go in affluence. They cannot go in affluence and apart apart with them this is why and width and said never said. At one time white black green blue with them with them with them you.

How can she not know that he he can with it that is with the most of having attended in the sense of waited.

There are three things. Not observant, not destined, not with relief.

There are many pleasures in store.

Next to no next to no no known known the same day the same day that that it was very interesting to not lose interest in it.

This leaves it once at once at once once left and right left and right left and right and insomuch there has been a mistake and really if really able to able to stop that.

It is more than originally left to me. Left to me. Left to me.

Leave it to you left to you left to right he had a good job and he left left right left.

A little in a little out and very often it is true when there is a possibility there are found very often it is true when there is a possibility they are found. Very often it is true when there is a possibility they are found.

Alright. When it is what is wanted what is it.

Always a little and always all always what is always with always always a hen always a chicken hen a chicken hen. A chicken hen a chicken, hen, a chicken a chicken hen always a chicken hen.

It is a very pleasant day. It is very pleasant to-day.

It is very pleasant. It is very pleasant to-day even if it is threatening that is if it is not absolutely as agreeable as far as weather is concerned as it was. It is very pleasant to-day and although the air is not light enough for much that is what is why they need food just the same. It is as pleasant here as it is any-where. It is pleasant when there is very much more than the time in which it is agreeable to choose the sound that is the one that is less the sound of wood than wood. Walking and working the sound of wood. This makes widening appealing. After all there are very many knives that have wooden handles. Also all especially and very much which is when there is a diversion.

What does having been very much as much as having been there mean to them.

Conversation can be how do you do.

How do you do.

How do you do.

Can harm harmful be with an exclusion of the part of the time in which they are carried. Carry him out but do not bend him. One five six three all out but she.

How does it have herds. Herds have heard it. With use.

Arthur and Arthur grass.

Begin now.

THE NOVEL

CHAPTER I

To bring them back to an appreciation of natural beauty or the beauty of nature hills valleys fields and birds. They will say it is beautiful but will they sit in it. This brings us to Lucy Church or Lucy Pagoda preferably Lucy Church. This brings to Lucy Church. The beauties of nature hills valleys trees fields and birds. Trees valleys fields flocks and butter-flies and pinks and birds. Trees fields hills valleys birds pinks butter-flies clouds and oxen and walls of a part of a building which is up. In cutting box wood there is no danger as box is a shrub which has a very agreeable odour. In placing it in an oven it is of very great use as it is not only Madeleine but Lucy Church who enjoys it. Not only Madeleine and Lucy and Therese Lucy Church who enjoys it. Who enjoys it. Markedly correcting the lack of necessity for coming and going admirably and she might. If two have left and there were four originally how many are there there now. Two and two make four. Anybody can say it was very good of them to stay and unexpectedly Therese came back and was of aid in indeed in in

and in the not the place of any one because every one was there is there. Very simply they made five better made five better than three made five of them of more use than three of them and this and disturbance. Let me see who can see, these replace those. And being forbidden to call all by the time by the time by the time by the time with fishes. Fishes in a lake. There might be very much preference between Therese's mother and George Elliot's mother and Henry Perrin's mother and it is lamentable if there is more care taken of where they went than a heavy cloud. Naturally a heavy cloud. Naturally. A heavy cloud. If they live together and then they had been offered what they had never asked to know as John and Eleanor would they be equal and uneasy in negation. This makes it moderately. And now allowed.

There is no difference between the country and the city between high hills and meadows in the bottom of the valley so she says. This with that withdrawn. Letting it have it. They are letting them have it. They are withdrawing whether it is once or twice or more than often. They imagine that after six days they are ready to receive anything. So they say. And around. What is it that is around what is it that is around them. More light from a coming to be added tower however they liked it. And they did. Everybody gave every effort and appreciated the result. And as it is as it is keeping as it is keeping as it is keeping as it is as it is as it is keeping it as

it is. There is no denial of the sound that they went up and down. A very strange idea. This is when when when might it might it have when when then by their chance with their dance and crowded. A whole number of them might be surprising.

Lucy Church additionally meant with it at all and having suddenly added number five to the number of those very well known here but not exactly.

Trading very well known here but not exactly.

Finally for them. Lucy Church and chickens she prefers fields to fields and she says so but necessity intervenes not necessity not obligation not assurance but the possibility of there being no neglect. Imagine she says. Imagine what I say.

Add cows to oxen goats to sheep and add cows and oxen and goats to sheep. Add oxen and cows and chickens and goats and sheep to fields and she will be satisfied so she says. She will be satisfied.

If more have named places in a cathedral in a very small quantity they are obliging.

That was why they were at work.

It has been said that clouds can meet but it has not been said whether the clouds were of the same size and thickness and never having seen it he said he wondered what it would be like and he was easily startled. So it would seem very likely they had to have it happen in order to let it be like that.

Bringing them back to liking to look at cumulus clouds quietly emerging behind the distant horizon. Cumulus clouds are very white when they are satis-

50

factory. From the standpoint of white they are very
satisfactory so they say otherwise they were satisfied.
He says he said that they returned. Could it be nearly
what is needed is needed with one some at a time.

No detaining Lucy Church to-day as she and they
are satisfied to be under obligation and very well I
thank you so they needed as much as before by that
time. Very many are older. How many are there
added with it. Three at a time and often one. If
every one hunts no one hunts. This is why they pray
and are successful successful that is they suddenly
withdraw once in a while where is it. After it is very
simply left to them it is very simply after it is very
simply left to them. They add years and left and
right and crosses and dishes. Why did they not come
and see the illumination. They did not come and see
the illumination of the other day and this makes it
be that it was a while a while here. Hear it as well
and very much what they should not state made it
do good to all of them Lucy Church makes it administer. Box bushes have a very agreeable odour when
they are dried and while they are drying.

She had no baby but that often happens when they
are excited and strong but she will have one.

It did not know its own hand writing but otherwise she was perfectly religious so she said. She said
alternately they were additional and he was older.
Very nearly more plans than indicated. If he were
here for eight days and during all that time he worked
so she says and it was as a result that they were very

pleased and they were complimented by very many and in addition by the bishop so they said there was every reason for their indifference and for the emptying of little by little all around. It was as an arrangement that made them not hesitate to stand and this could they very many so she says could they, so she said with a mixture of embellishment.

Might be very natural for them to dip them in colour.

Lucy Church was amiable and very much resuscitated. She was amiable and she was amiable and she was very much resuscitated.

They were these things were an argument in favour of being very much which makes it not unlikely to give directly to them when it is more than told and she said very likely they were winning. John Mary and hour glasses which are the same as clocks striking or at least theirs as much. He was lonely and was leaving when the time had come to leave he was leaving. It is an amiable understanding to buy what is left from left to right.

They might be all as much used to it and so they argued who made them dilate of the sacredness of letting it be known as having received much of it. Much of it in time. Who to whom with when and he said very much has been told very differently. Lucy Church made an authority of being vexed when they were able to state that Josephine was not very well. And all of it allowed out loud and beside that in preparation and beside that William and Elizabeth did not

condone not having been very much in believing that it is not particularly at a distance toward which they are looking. Some say something. And do not like it. How many days are there in it so she says and by the time they are afraid he has learned to be more of it as much. With them. There are many remaining with them.

Every time it makes it be all of it very nice and quiet I thank you there is a new explanation. Once it was the banker and once it was some one who was present. Very nice and quiet I thank you. Lucy Church made no difference to recompense as theirs allowed. Lucy Church fastened the whole very well as she would as she said as she said ultimately as she said. Lucy Church and John Mary with violence if to come quickly is to come at all and just at all very much as if with them with it as in case could Lander be the same name as Landor. She said it could.

What happened to them. They said they were sorry but they were afraid she was not intelligent enough to disguise herself.

What happened to them.

They were not mentioned again and so although it is known to them and to others what happened to them it is not known it is not known what happened to them.

How is it not known what happened to them. It is not known what happened to them. In a conversation it was not known what happened to them. In a recitation it was not known what happened to them.

In a description it was not known what happened to them. In attention it was not known what happened to them. Thereby when they were unusually disappearing it was not known what happened. It was not as known what happened to them. They made a wide investigation so she said. They did not know what had happened to them. Very often they will know what has happened to them but they are mistaken. Ivory is mistaken. They do not ask but it is told fortunately it is told to them it is told them what happened to them. They knew what had happened to them. They had gone that way and were in contact with others who would know what happened to them and as widely. More often as widely.

They were left to place themselves in their excuse and so also also as a retrial of a river that has been as wide as often and as often which is why there is a width which is theirs where they do regret their being there last. She said she added anything and correctly.

Lucy Church is not annoyed by salt and security not at all as beside which they know that there is a very welcome Mary. John Mary in case of a difference between how old very many autographs are. Autographs are signatures with a pencil very well I thank you. And so must you go. Plenty plenty of sun on shoes. This is as plainly as poplar trees in crucifix. There are some who expect only one child and some who expect a number. Let it go as well as if it is there hope. They hope.

Suppose eight more are cactuses and have rosy

flowers. They do not grow with the same pleasure as when there are when there is an interval in between. Letting it be just as bye the way Therese how are you now that you have done just what has been expected. Done and Yvonne how many trees are there on it on the property where there is a very excellent hope that she will be the embodiment of laughter and would it be at all. Not to give her pleasure. Attached to me so she said and very correctly. A circumstance by which Lucy Church profited.

There is this difference between a chicken a pig and a central tower that they are at a distance and very nearly heard. How is it. She is in the hope of instant transition from red to easier and from there to there. They made identical twins easily. And do they say so. They do she likes do.

Do do she likes do.

They said when it is all said and a perennial which means hot houses a perennial with a wish. Wish on a wish bone so she says. Albert Church so she says was welcome so she says. She said Albert Lionel Winthrop was religious cultivated and an inventor of toys which are made here and sold there. He said that once in a while he was told. And so with wider. A transition of vinegar and oil mixed with olives almonds and if you would if you would be so kind. Elizabeth Church very lately. A duty which she did was this she turned from right to left and from left to right and fell asleep. What is the difference between Lucy Church and Alice as they did not meet. They were

an integral instance of representation and their equivalent. And how seen how seen mean collected between
coloured lean with their enjoyment never in the day
when it is abandoned and when abandoned and then
or relaxing with standing belvedere.

And she was conscious of the effort so she said very
well and thank you for the pleasure of their return.
Lucy Isabel Arthur Wilfred Louise Blanche Violet
Frederick Eugene Martin and Eli so she said were so
she said Dorothea so she said ingrained. A table cloth and
will and hunting. It is very easily opened at a place.
Hours of contentment and their after all will they do it.

The moon is what is seen in the day-light. A church
by church or church with church for church might
church allowed a church to be there. Here there and
everywhere every one will take a dare. A dare is
something which they have forgotten. Forget forgotten
allowed to collect rain-water. And now at last.

Lucy Church is wealthy and might be what she
wished but as every one is wealthy and might be what
she wished Lucy and every one is wealthy and might
be what she wished. Wished and won. Hours and
hours and hours of glass come to see the undivided
interest. There is great interest in clouds fields valleys mountains poplars and intermediate passers by
who are engaged in manual labour which is why they
are surrounded pleasantly with very well I thank you
in case in case of permanent. She said she was understood as an allowance of she had never been there.
She had never been there.

CHAPTER II

Two and two make four. Four and four make eight. Eight and eight make sixteen and sixteen and twelve make twenty-eight.

Lilies lily they have avoided partially why. Supposing two met at once which one was the one that it was decided might love what is there where there is as much there as much there and there in a way there there with never to like later later than it is. John Mary with no reason for being with them with them with with them.

There is nothing more explaining than having water supplied water supplied water supplied she and he both said waggoning. It was in and by never have a pillar of as a pleasure because it would countenance coutenance that. There is no difference whether he looks like Simon or whether he does not.

Simon when and fall Simon Church out loud. Simon Ethel out loud. Simon Edith out loud. Simon William out loud. Simon Elizabeth out loud. Simon Couttall out loud. Simon Charles Simon with it Simon very well Simon Alice very well I thank

you. Simon South who went about and said it is very nicely evident that they exchange wire for west and it is their pleasure. It is the pleasure of the very different difference every afternoon after noon. Arthur Church Hardy Church Charles Church and Angelica Church and Simon James and Simon Alvaro and Simon Emanuel. It can easily hit the head. When all is said it can easily hit the head.

Parties of two means that if one slept and one was careful not to waken the one that slept what would Lucy Church say. By the way what would Lucy Church say. Lucy Church was very much attracted by the arrangement that had been made for October. It is always a mistake for the sun to come through the window from within to the outside.

It is a little day to-day it is a little day to-day it is a little day to-day it is a little day to-day. It is very easy to be asked to be at a time. One at a time.

Eighty four makes sixty two and what do they do about it. They are annoyed not by interruption but by past time.

Please to plainly wishing to go home home to your home.

She was in part and they say, Lucy Church made stables stables be boarded up.

To have stopped if she had awakened but she did not awake and so although she was awake although she wakened power through repose and chose. There she said there is a difference between chose and choose.

There may be war but there can be no climaxes there.

Unaccountably.

With when when it is as much as they had had.

Having had had having had she did not waver.

Lucy Church unaccountably adaptably and with their attitude of speedy departure. One has left one is to leave in october one is to leave at first in September and the other is not to leave at all as she says so. Leave coming to to the day after the first Simon Hardy. The first Simon Coolidge and their addressor. Everybody has wealth as narrowly as in a door. As in a door so she says might it be with it as the same elaborately.

Lead it by theirs which is why every little change is changes. She said with very much to have to be and very quietly to be to see and with undoubtedly to rest and prepare prepare matches and candles if the electricity should go out and he heard completeness with ease.

Completeness with ease.

It is why is it very much as much as with them left to it in this finally as an instance directly they might very quietly admire as they came outwardly to them in them with them will he come again running.

She said that a pagoda and chains a church and places and window and extra ruins and a name makes it be comfortably what is it when they are very frank. Nobody is interested in a neglected child.

Lucy Church, John Mary and Simon Marguerite.

They might be unknown. Lucy Church John Mary and Simon Therese they might be unknown as yet and yet and yet they might be known as men women and children fields distance and dissuaded they may be known as mixing oil with salt water and not all at once also as being wealthy very much and very quiet and very well I thank you. They might be known by their saying something about a right of way. Away was made perfectly possible and perfectly practicable and if by this as an indication of their reverence they do decline to colour white to mauve and blue red white and blue all out but you so she says. Quietly so she says and by by and by. Very much as it was it was as she said. Correctly stated as she said.

Lucy Church one two three. It is astonishing as she says that it will stay longer. There has never been a suspicion that there is a difference between open and closed. Lucy Church made master-pieces readily and excitedly.

John Mary in August and John Mary in August and in July and John Mary made it do as a difference between fourth and sixth and with a place. A place where you can tell that it is earlier or later is very desirable and very desirable. John Mary is very desirable by this time. John Mary shouter. John Mary win and winsome winsomeness are easily seen and he was disappointed as he had expected what he saw.

She said to Virgil do come and be useful.

He said to Virgil do come.

It is by out loud and a cloud that snow persists.

Persists is in twos and threes and poplars and please. Please be careful of their measure.

They may deceive you.

If they do bring what is brung what have you there. So she says.

There is a difference between a name and where they went to have lunch luncheon and until until it was left to be like that.

A bird with a long tail on a bush.

What does the barometer do it tells the truth to me and to you.

Arguments of fair weather.

If added peaches grow on grow on grow on walls walls if added peaches grow on walls Wednesday Lucy Alice Church will laugh and say Wednesday. And this is why they admire trees and with this trees and with this bees bees are harmless and bees with this bees with this are harmless and made it be their life. Lucy Church and John Mary and Simon Therese and Lindo Webb wish bone and are frightened by excellent set of pairs of let and letting it yet be an in contrast to their shown having it mark a place. Yes do. And though. Though might mind it as more with as made as if with called hawk or or letting it a piece of their inland inland includes the sea. See Susy. Lucy Church established this as all. All yet. Lucy Church made merry. Merry del Val. Remaining intrenched in their left to right mountain meadow with rim. It is very likely so she says and they were in the middle of the most endurable and therefor their pleasure

pleasing please and she said they were more than there had been.

Not to be aided.

Tells well bell if a cow bell were a bell as well and meditative. Lucy Church looked at it and was not presently particularly withstood. Fairly well I thank you. Lucy Church might be that if seen it will come here might be if in seen and will come here. Lucy Church has in in women. Lucy Church could mediaevally speaking have a glass and see in the distance that there is elegantly speaking what there is to detach. A building from until and a chain from throw and a tree from there and a cloud from allowed. It is very nearly their aptitude for send her.

Come and close it.

It is very nearly their aptitude for Mr. Armandine and in between it is very nearly their aptitude for recently with it there.

Very nearly their aptitude. Alice Church vigilantly Lucy Church vigilantly John Mary vigilantly Simon Therese vigilantly Simon Marguerite vigilantly Arthur Part vigilantly Lucy Church vigilantly Simon Therese vigilantly John Mary vigilantly Alice Church vigilantly Simon Marguerite vigilantly Arthur Part vigilantly.

Having never forgotten in and add adder.

It is theirs in hope.

How can forward and back slowly and turn around be surprising readily. Readily. Readily. How can

readily be forward and back slowly and be surprising turn around readily.

Many change more churn whether gather they are best. The most worth while of them all. What is the difference between swallows pigeons edible birds hawks and plays. They are all across. A consecrated cross of surprise that it can be seen a man a wagon and an oxen team. How are they known as it when they do not move how are they known as it when they do not move. They are certainly known as it when they do not move.

When they do move there are as many as they were and they do move. As they do move out of sight as they do move. At it.

Lucy Church additionally Lucy Church. Meant and intended and gathered and attended to it.

To save Edward.

Edward Elden.

Charles Elliot.

William William.

And their part.

Partly a chance to be with well known apart. Whether. Lucy Church whether Lucy Church whether it is a gain Lucy Church whether it is a gain that Lucy Church suddenly seldom saves pagodas and Italy. So she says. Allowed it so she says. Variably so she says. Advantageously so she says.

It does not make any difference when the difference between a poplar and a fig tree is ascertained.

On account of white.

Lily lily who has the lily.
Fern fern who has the fern.
Fern fern who has the fern.
Lily lily who has the lily.
There is no need of mentioning names.
There to be very earnestly adding.
Not that but always a pleasure.
Merchandise always a pleasure. Not wealth but always a pleasure.
With them and always a pleasure.
Added additionally left to be pleased as pleased. Always a pleasure.

Simon Therese might address Simon Therese might address and might caress. Always a pleasure. Lucy Church very seldom interrupts as if it were that if there were never a confusion between on the withstood articulation of preparation and Lucy was mistaken. She did not leave she was advantageously surrounded as she was and it was surmounted a church was surmounted by a pagoda and illustrated by a crown of red blue and pretty lights. And so if it were possible it was possible to go away. She said if it had been arranged to go away and went away. Lucy Church made mountains which are perpetually covered with snow that is to say no deception as it is when it is down there. Down always means nearer. Simon Therese is very careful to dot his eyes and to close his ears and to declare his succession to those that follow and wish to plan one day in the month. Simon Marguerite is as very sweetly shouldered as if he were

ascertained to be very likely with them. John Mary having shut the door opened it again but not always sometimes it had to be done for him. The difference between the present and the past. Pastime.

Every one now.

From the standpoint of white white like a cloud a white cloud white like the snow white snow white like the white sun white sun white like the lily a white small lily that is like embroidery, white like anything made white which is readily white and not often changed to an other colour. White not often changed to an other colour. This is with an integral part of with it now.

Simon Therese made a face and he said I might be made to be another time with them.

Lucy Church individually. John Mary wealthy and very much whether it was by the time that they had their observation of how butterflies flew. It is very lamentable to have them know the name very lamentable.

What happened to William Williams. He was not what was more than theirs. And Henry Henry. He danced. And George John. He was not only not very well but very much at home wherever he is.

There is no pleasure in coversation.

And is used.

She counted the leaves and there were more of them than she had expected would be left. Counted the leaves and there were more than she expected would be left.

Disappearing.

If it is chosen to be an earring disappearing.

If it is chosen with a worth the pleasure of having denied an observation and at length three or two not about with the place of theirs in waiter. Wait await her. She and mean I mean I mean wait and wait and retreating from very much that has been returned has had the covering removed and at last and as there never had been any glass in the windows before eighteen forty two or thereabouts so she says.

It is very strangely that three does not make four. Remember a tree remember three three to a tree three a tree three trees poplars as well as fruit trees a peach tree in a vine or a land tree will be fine. It is very well to prevent wishes.

Lucy Church had chosen a very pretty place and very pretty views and very pretty very pretty to choose and very pretty to use and very pretty very pretty to close and very pretty in place of places. A very pretty selection of their arrival.

And more than after a while. Every day a thousand and every other day a thousand and three and every other day a thousand and three everywhere.

Lucy Church might be very much as she wished to decide that that bread can change and with it at all and with it at all and made of it at once.

Who knows the difference between once and twice and John Mary interchanges left to right. Interchanges. Very quickly interchanges might leave it to them with them he leaving with them with them

in place of eight and forty two. It is very noticeable that if she sits and rests it is very much a very great pleasure to observe her.

2.30, 3.30, 4.30, 5.30, 6.30, 7.30, 8.30. It is not easy to be seen wishing when the water is noisy.

Lucy Church does not introduce subjects.

Subject places.

John Mary has quietly been outlined.

Poplars and places.

Simon Therese understands medals and four places. With this as that.

Lucy Church marries marries with when with when what is the difference between vines and shrubs.

At last and last and last to go.

There are two things for not watching she says there is one thing for not watching she says there is one thing for not watching. There are two things for not watching.

Derange the service so he said and not fishing so he said and solved with pleasure so he said and golden rod and was very visible and in great abundance and not now and by the time and with it diminishing and might be when as seen so and so much as and as much with and whether whether repeated he ever went to be nearly very much advised as to their being very nearly at once favourably suitable to their joining their delight in with within estimate and allusion to pond lilies.

They made it be partly adroit.

There is no doubt about one thing it happens one

at a time and in between they wait for flowers for plainly established interjections and because of this. Two kinds of arrivals mean milk bread. A conversation about milk bread which is a monologue. Milk bread is not variable and it is variable and if there is pretentiouness not only will not the ones desired not be chosen but in a choice in a very nearly unnatural choice and with it with it as an elegance. Eglantine and deadly night shade and mistaken. Lucy Church in hyperbole.

John Mary more manifest and meant made it be left to them when when with it as a best in time left lightly. He made it be. Might they be right when they say that every day is with them an applicable and much attended with mischance and with their value. And with it or ordinarily their being a difference between fast flowing and fast flowing.

There is no encampment in their care.

Leave let her ride. Lucy Church was more than ever when they tried.

Lucy leave it to them. Lucy leave it to them but very well more than he or she can tell and they will they will tell that it is attributable to them that this is at once at once and at once and shown and at once left to the next with it as an immaculate successfulness of with and when and is and can can this with it for foremost Simon Therese and letting it leave this as a trace.

An orange bee on pink clover and a white butterfly flying very well and high over the center of a wide river.

It is not imaginable that they mind this.

One two three four five six seven eight nine ten eleven twelve thirteen times as high.

They are right jewelry is the most pleasurable so he says.

They made a division of fives.

He made a division of six.

She made a division of seven.

All good children go to heaven.

He made a division of two.

She made a division of five.

They made a division of their having lifted it. He made a division of every once in a while and John Mary of course. John Mary of course.

He made a division of indecision and it was at night at most at best and with it as if in Aspinwall where they arranged to have in a manner of adding with it as before when there is with it and renewing the sudden interruption of their being a difference between paper and birds.

She does does she.

It is an indicated soon that she is within within the room after she has been with without noon without soon with within within soon it is an indicated noon within soon.

As she does was and very very very crisis very tell all in illustration do and does and deter dance. A glance at the pleasure of pleasure of sent a plant planted with letting, and nothing not must with let it field in cows and how and house. Not in repair.

With with a very best left to it now how now.

Lucy Church is very impressed by having been very much and very pleasantly surrounded by what she feels and felt to be very much what is desirable and that is pleasantly. Having three as far apart makes it be pardonable to not when needed have moving and also giving blue to green and thought thought with that there for this comically. Choose choose through through the left to it and he did not say so and so. A little jerk a little turk and a little Spaniard sitting on around makes a forest fire entirely when it is where they are and three are satisfied not to be there.

Very pale blue in the distance very pale blue in the distance very pale blue in the distance and she says she agrees to it to that.

There is a very great happiness in not doing it twice. Twice is once.

If a very dark made silver to be bought by the pound is a very tall made poplar to be very much below and it is to have hidden a long way away from a white in all an elevation and there is more around than they encourage whose has it to be more than with it that in the same name as when he would on three sides have it changed to consume consummate changing left to right and very nice and quiet I thank you.

He is astounded.

Letting theirs be once in a while encouraged.

The cause of conversation is this seated on the

chair and by wide by side by retied by letting it be
belied and so he said church he said pagoda he said
briefly he said well yet and very much as a mountain
and time her and yet he said he said he had visited
the picture gallery of the city which had been represented continuously as having been won and won. Won
and won. Two be with this.

Conversation in left and right. There is no doubt
that it is very often applicable to have a ribbon upon
a pin very often applicable.

There is no doubt that won wonderfully short
shortly and with with it is in an ineradicable they and
circumstance with this and allowed. She might be
as a care.

There is doubtless a difference between five in one
year and one in every once in a while or one in an
interval of more than a year more than a year and so
he said. More than one year.

Conversation who does who does do who can and
does do the best that is to be seen wonderfully attitude
as this and sitting on a chair each on a chair sitting
each on a chair.

Conversationally how conversationally how what
is the difference between oxen and a cow between a
deer and a goat between a wagon and a plough between
left and right between fields and counting and between
a hunt and as many having him when he came he came
to say that cathedrals are plainly visible at one time
as well as houses as well as well he says that it is not
at all difficult left and lift not at all difficult lift and

left and left and lift not at all difficult that they plan this on a day when they say the first day he came to stay the second day in memory of the third day the third day the day in which it is better to wish than not and so three days are holidays and four days are four days. When this you see remember me. She said when this you see remember this remember when this you see remember that it was at most at best at best and when this you see to be to be that it is never what she says what she says what she says Paul she says Therese she says. She does not say Paul Henry nor does she say Simon Therese nor does she say very well does she say the sun is not shining that way this way this way she does say that way she does she can say can say stabilised she can say additionally she can say pointedly she can say do say we say they say and say say so.

Lucy Church makes ploughs famous and makes ploughs famous and makes ploughs famous and makes ploughs famous as they are famous as they are famous as they as they are as they are famous Lucy Pagoda makes ploughs famous as ploughs are famous as they are famous.

If bread is eaten and sugar to sweeten how many are as well as said.

She saw and no more.

And hours.

There is not much conversation in abundance.

How much conversation is there in abundance.

Lucy Church and follows.

There is no difference in at their side.

Lucy Church in abundance there is the difference there is a difference and at the side.

Three things together. Cows ploughs and ferry-boats. A mountain is very well I thank you.

She made it be be buy and or or pears. She made it do do do or few few or theirs. She made it left left left right left or care care for it. He says that when he is not thoughtful about fish and waiting then as a result he does not find any very small daisies as he can see in the grass very readily. And it is not at all presently that in between a screen if it is asked for and it is there there is an attention to it an attention to it with it all.

Come to see the pears which are extraordinarily large and long and juicy so he says extraordinary large and long so she says extraordinary large and long so he says. A plan to have a number of them a plan to have a number of them a plan to have a number of them a plan to have a number of them a plan to have a number of them.

It would be very well if a kitten would need to have it given to them as food to feed as if it had it as a need to have it and seed a seed sown there is very well pleased if it makes no difference at one time one at a time she said one at a time and in recently recently reverberation with it at all. Who knows potatoes and tomatoes and pears and leaves and please and if in indeed trees.

A continued waiting might be if three crowded around.

Lucy Church could be more than beside with them.

John Mary with them beside with them.

Simon Therese with them went sent with them sent it with them.

Lucy Church with them with them Lucy Church went sent with sent went with sent went with them sent them with them went with them. Lucy Church made it have it with it as it Lucy Church with it sent it in this having come from here he had with very little more than having been here and not left. Left and right.

Lucy Church made a part of it by this and that with it having Miss Buckingham not be lined with fur. Far and farther. There is every difference between John Mary and Simon Therese in perpetuity.

CHAPTER III

To change from there to this that is two cooks to two cooks to two cooks to there to this and surrounded. Anybody surrounded by maids is surrounded by maids to there to this. Two cooks to there to this. Surrounded by maids Lucy Church surrounded by surrounded by surrounded by with them in them surrounded by surrounding they not with them in in best to have the best and most and best first. Two cooks to them to them two cooks to them and they they were in the stenghth of having had a land to see and fell and well and beside to rest to return to plant and make a ground and with a tree four six plane trees which give a shade but not nearly here. Two cooks very well to do it to do it by this by that and never have had that desirably and with Mary fairly fairly very nice and quiet I thank you.

Two make two. Two make four. And a little it was asked and why no more.

A wealthy cook who owns very much prefers to fight simply for his country rather than be protected from danger and terror and in this way when they

return each separately were very wealthy and very much as often as up and down and they were not delighted.

Lucy Church says admirably be pleased to be instructive. And they were believing that at some distance forty towns were not so many. Forty towns were not so many forty two forty two towns. Could she who had borne four children speak as she did to one who having borne two would bear two more. They never met.

Do you like if they are well to be so much with that and think and with it claim that they can do that they have lost that in the most that with the felt and might it be that is the share that is at least at least at most and can be had to be had to be on the head.

Very much as they were had and thank you very nice and quiet I thank you.

What is when they search for the time when if the grass is high if the grass is high do mushrooms grow in the grass if the grass is high not if the grass is very high and pleases. There is widening of reverberation of accompanying pleases with pleases.

Lucy Church is an example of upholding upholding upholding this as their advantage. Lucy Church is an example of upholding of upholding of upholding box as hedge as their advantage Lucy Church is an example of upholding of their upholding of their upholding of upholding this as an advantage. Lucy Church is an example of their upholding this as an advantage.

Lucy Church come to to the best of Timothy the best of Timothy and there find mushrooms there find mushrooms and there have a stick which has been cut around so that the bark having been taken off in such a way it matches matches pleases presses and the best known method of looking is when there is the sun on the head. Sun on the head and said said sun said sun on said sun on the said sun on the head.

They gradually came nearer to Godiva so he said and he had observed it.

Coming to have forty waiting forty waiting forty waiting as if for instance we all wait forty waiting as if for instance we all went.

Lucy Church made pressing a pressing reason for pressing them to join in join in as if they were comforting in saying no more came.

Lucy Church was with them when John Mary John Mary was the brother of a younger James Mary who would come and be if it were to be what was to be needed by seeing oxen oxen are not lost if they walk faster and of course they do.

Nobody knows that wild pinks are carnation colour. If they do they have never mentioned it.

Simon Therese would find it unavoidable to see when Elizabeth well very well.

All this makes them fourteen be three.

How old is the mother of five and another. The oldest seventeen not very much younger the youngest two not very much younger. The youngest the young-

est not very much younger and who calls whom. They do not disturb him at all at all not at all.

How many grow an apple tree when there has been very much rain. How many like what they come to ask is it ask is it. Lucy Church avoided avoided crows which are blue. Crows which are blue. A quality of crows which are blue.

Lucy Church and Lucy Pagoda on the border of a river and the river is wider when there has been very much rain. Thank you.

This are as well as ever in addition.

This is as well as ever in addition.

No and nicely.

What does an out of door dinner consist in eaten at noon. Of very much that has packed and repacked. For what has there been given for which there has been more than there was. Fruit which was not forgotten. What can be avoided if better can be procured. Cake and bread. What is the significance of their pleasing themselves. A little with all that is what is not only more than is which is when the moistened safety of their alone and they were delighted to be in at once rejoined for this and with it as an independence of their allowing. She said it was meant to be one at a time.

Are partly are partly are partly left.

Nora is not a name that I have preferred nor is Dora a name that I have preferred. Ida is a name that I have preferred and Ivy is a name that I have preferred preferred to it.

John Mary John Mary who is to be the best of

three. John Mary Simon Therese and James Mary who is to be the best of three John James Mary who is to be the best of three. James Mary James Mary who is to be the best of three John Mary Simon Therese James Mary James Mary Simon Therese John Mary who is to be the best of three.

Lucy Church did not have a mother when she was a mother and grandmother. Lucy Church was never a mother and that was because there was a difference of between two in three.

To change Lucy Church from Lucy Church Lucy Church. One two and one two and one two and one two.

There have been many statues and would there be many statues statues have never been named renamed. Lucy Church fortunately.

Lilian Anne St Peter Stanhope met in winter.

This is the day when it was written as they say correctly and she was felt and freely to be asked would he stay and he was after all pleased that he had not gone away.

It was very pleasant there were a number there listening and very few of them were proved to be which it is admirably aroused and pleased pleased pleasantly with their concurrence.

Lucy Church was not there. She was at that time in the midst of knowing that easily and looking the best and varied in arising from which it is with them as it is to leave it as it is that the variation of their addition might if it could be with them and under-

taken a very nicely changed freshet. And so meadows can have lilies lilies mauve and a surprise. It is not a surprise if it is brought here.

Lilian Ann St. Pierre might visit us here. And it would be a pleasure and after speaking of the weather would it if it were fruitful could there be a companion of a very edible everything and a very edible thing a very edible everything which is partly their remark and remarkable they are remembered for their everything at one time and not too much and inasmuch admirably.

This pleases threes and fives and one very often one very often one one to three.

In this and subdued. In this and subdued and added and subdued and added and added and added added and subdued.

There is no caution in mowing green clover with a protection. Clover always has a colour rose, red, pale, blue, green and something delightful and foreseen. It does not seem useless to look again.

Simon Therese John Mary James Mary who has been to this and left it when it was not where it had been with the time with which it was chosen as if it had been ineradicable and suspected of a change. They might be as they were with more than is left to them to determine with half and on behalf of it. It is remarkable that there is more than there is if it is in a pressure of their announcement of how often and with which it is if a disappointment and not be he had here. If it is not to be given here where is it to be

given. Mary Worthington only said of it that it was not what had been found to be with and with it at all as for the celebration of their identity with the rest of the obligation to be reached. They were perfectly in accord and very many hoped and very many hoped that at one end there was protection and protecting of what they had and at the other end there was consumption and consuming of what they had. Both indeed both indeed and both indeed. It might be that having hitherto and before two having hitherto two and having before having been well well into into the midst of their attack and attention attack and attention. Who is whose. A number a number of preparation. Mushrooms if they are fresh and very small and wild are always delicious particularly if they grow in fields and not near trees nor woods.

CHAPTER IV

She was right about thunder a threshing machine
and left and right but not about turning to the left
before crossing the river. She said that it was very
delightful to receive pleasantly illustrations of Paul
and Virginia.

Bright and light candle-light it would be very an-
noying if they were not replaced. This was not said
of Duchess pears or indeed of Williams. Lucy Church
made arrangement to have tube-roses not found in as
great a quantity as desired. John Mary was present
when there was question of part and a part of what
was wanted and also the two who had seen and had
been made to indulge in favourable comment upon
their delight in anticipation more breathlessly eager
to have light shown though coloured glass and in this
way it was a pleasure as well as a prophecy to say so.

A count might ask what had they to do with it.
It might very well be partly James Mary partly James
and Mary James Mary partly. partly what they did.
It is very different to have rain and to see rain so he
said and he added it is very different to guard cows

and corn stalks than it is to grow admittedly cymbals. It is very well known that they are often as an honour. In order to honour him. Very admittedly often an honour in order to honour him. Simon Therese Lilian Ann St Peter and Lilian Ann St Peter Stanhope might easily indicate in front and in back of the rest of their observance and of course.

Lucy Church can administer as well as Josephine partly as they care to have it offered to them.

Lucy Church hoping to be startling. Lucy Church felt as an illumination. Lucy Church practically wishing that she might have been as fortunate as she was.

What does he say he says that after all it is not only that mountains differ differently and meadows differ differently and rivers differ differently and bells differ differently and poplars differ differently but also that paper differs differently and allowance differs differently and their continued fragrance differs differently. At last and at most and as well as joined. It is very nearly deplorable that a young woman loves to be very well met very well met very well met that a very much younger child hopes that there is more desire than can be upheld by a purchase and that a very young priest has been met once and as often as if he had been allowed at least that it is by them politely and partly and with it as a reestablishment of their individual recognition of very young and finally as old neglecting this for that. It is by no means what they said that made them place it as if it could be as much as coming to be anticipated should it be shown. Hav-

ing heard it as they could be sure to know. Known and with it integrally theirs seen. Believing shown as might it be known, slowly, an older wishing and to cross and perhaps ostentatiously not having it advance by having it withheld from crossing. To say so. Lucy Church has thanked.

They know so much they do they like to have it though, with.

They had to have to stay and they chose to let it come to-day. Very likely once in a while. They were very much more than expected.

If it is when it is pears peaches and grapes plums apples and figs north or south in summer set or winter.

It is palatable that it is very much more easily done that there is occasion for their being intended to have looked and left it to them. What do they dislike most. Not having what is given to them.

Lucy Church said that she found it unpleasant to have marble under her hand. Marble is frequently very like wood. Wood is frequently very like silver silver is frequently very like in vain.

Books in porcelain mentioned the first time as an incident.

Lucy Church was very well yesterday.

It is to be added and expected added and expected that René John Etienne Ernest and their cousin who is additionally older should be seated and with them the little one Annette and her governess who had dark rims around as if they were large glasses and it is very dark and it might have been added but it was

natural and in a way as she was young and very much as if not only pleasant but attentive could be.

Lucy Church made mountains out of mole hills. They are by and by as if they were having asked having asked having asked of her descendant.

Leaves and leaves and leaves leaves and leaves and leave and leave and leave and leave it leaves and leaves and leaves and leaves and leaves it.

It is by the way by the way taught by the way thought thought by the way thought it is thought by the way thought that conscription that a colonel that made of following and that having been asked and having asked for it they would could and should respect his prejudices.

Would it be pleasant to recognise what they mean. He said it would be pleasant to recognise what they mean. He said it would be he said it would be pleasant to recognise what they mean.

John Mary does not definitely prepare to leave it to his brother James Mary to do. He has had every intention of finally betrothing himself to Estelle Geneveray but in the meantime it is apparent apparently that he is inclined to be circuitous and in this as in a way if within waiting he might if she were at least after more readily having announced a future she might be more often than ever theirs at once which when went again could it be round about. John Mary is in hope that the weather will change and make lakes as well as rivers more as they were and if they are more

as they were there would be no outcome to the left and right provisionally.

It is very often that tapering candles are in very small blue candlesticks.

She said that it was quite useless to watch clouds but she was quite mistaken in this way there is every reason to be optimistic and playful and hopeful and determined and partly at that time.

Lucy Church might mention whistles.

Lucy Church is in a way as if to say come again and be here on time.

Simon Therese uniquely has been ill he has been the next to the youngest of ten children of whom all of them are well and prosperous his mother extremely good looking and well to do and he himself in every way inclined to be an inspiration to the most difficult question of might it be just as well. He might be very often as and in preparation for the more advantageous allowance of why they should be left at once.

Lucy Church an authority.

What could they say when they met to-day they could say that they were very much pleased with the arrangement not that had been made but with the unexpected addition to their society in spite of the fact that they had said that they had anticipated it in conversation. Very likely in time. Lucy Church was inclined to prefer water falls or rather the pouring out of a small but violently running stream over a small amount of obstruction and so running into the main

current as so many mouths in effect of which it is continually opposite.

Lucy Church in reasonably at first.

This time it is true.

Going to go on.

Did she ever see a bear climb a greased pole.

Going to go on.

One or two or one or two.

Did she ever see two take two.

He had a very pleasant interest in eating bread.

He had a very decided liking for watching.

He had a very impatient way of after all looking at lightning when it was accompanied by what after all made it very much after all what made it after all that they would stay there and wait.

Eight and Lucy Church.

Eight and very likely.

If one goes up it is to be presumed that they all go up.

It is very easy to know that the rattling of paper means the making of packages and entirely at their beck and call not at all not more than not at all. It is said by one who is in a position to observe that luncheon should be called a dinner and should be partaken with with and of with with and of with with with with with and of, it should be and here where the evening is tranquil tranquil that is to say if there is neither rain nor sun if there is neither rain nor sun it is in that case tranquil and there is no necessity for having often called them to eliminate anything. A rainbow promises.

CHAPTER V

Lucy Church was left alone as much as if there could be very many ways to have theirs be their own and she went she was very often at one time which is very nearly what is at least might be at more than half of that in place of their needing this because the best of it is whether this and that nearly left to it in the meantime as they came. Lucy Church creditably and because if so and trout and because if so and trout and because if so and inundation in a meadow inundation in a meadow.

Inundation in a meadow is different from inundation in a marsh a marsh can be small very small and high very high and very prettily so. A marsh can be felt to be their gift.

Lucy Church was in one at a time and meant to be pleasantly in place of having it this time and once at a time once at a time and not left when they were to them. Lucy Church is indebted to rain for her belief in white and pink. Pink and it might be when it is ordinarily theirs to be sure. It is not only because but with it at once that they choose them and say how

88

do you do. A father quite as much a father quite as much and she quite as much a father quite as much.

Simon Therese can never be an additional pleasure to them an additional with this as old as old as if if it is it is like that.

Be told.

One one one two three, three one three one two three. It is a deception.

Every day in which very many come very many come. Every day in which very many come there is beside that they say where shall we go to stay where shall we go to stay. It is believed to be ineradicable that they are very often here every once in a while. They said what makes it be simple that they need it as a provision.

He resembles him in this light.

Lucy Church answered that it was true it was not a beginning or an end it was neither the one or the other.

It is very peculiar.

It is very peculiar.

There should be both a rise and a cessation so there should.

John Mary so there should. James Mary Lucy Church Simon Therese Lilian St. Peter and those to whom they were to be more cordial as time went on. It is by this time.

Not a Polish bride nor a hollander beside can lakes be emptier and more full.

And Lucy Lucy let Lucy let Lucy can let Lucy can

can let Lucy if it is crystal on the road and traversed can wait and passage instil fear.

And so Lucy and so bringing and so down and so a hill and so with better and so having refused to be attested as as provide provided letting it as a valley and cascade beside the next to a room in which there may be a bevy of theirs in better than if this and be in choice of left it to them with. Could it be better done won one and one one should never be replied as two and two if too and light it now with out more ado.

In place of strange.

Complicated horses now. Horses now cow now complicated horses now. Horses now horses and a cow now. Complicated horses now.

It is torn in between and shells egg shells it is best as yellow peaches with a rose rosy rosy green.

Lucy Church an advantage Lucy Church made by it being with them it is attempting with them attempting with them. And might it be that that good good good if if it is not a bee or a wind a bee is from there and the wind is from there and so sheep so sewn so seated so when and then then so so much as much as withdraw.

Lucy Church made it seem that Grenoble was far away.

Listen to Lucy.

Lucy Church made a church made a church Lucy Church.

Lucy Church win win and win with and with with win.

Lucy Church made safely safely with plans and might it be on the other side from that on which it came down and was as much like water as anything.

Lucy Church has had to have theirs to day to say. She said she said it is why they ask me to be so good as to ask it of them that that that it is is it what is more left than right and so is a moon soon and it has been arranged from the twenty-sixth to the first so the calendar says.

Leave completing completing it to them if they have mushrooms in fields mushrooms in fields so they have said of it of them of very well of them of very well of them.

In there a month what have they said they have said that they are withstood and with and stood and surfeited with some and settle. Settle and settlement was always as late. Now there are he said now there are three in a year and at that time there were five in every part of once a year and so much and as much and with it and much as it could could should and treated as if they they were they were to go in snow. It is very agreeable to have been with them if they were flushed with sun suddenly.

Simon Therese in case Simon Therese in case in case of not having been where where were they.

Simon Therese was met as he was coming down the hill carrying a pail of water in order to bring it carrying as if a chinaman carrying as if a chinaman were judging and pleasantly perfectly perfectly pleasantly it

was within three. Three times and out. Out out with it.

Simon Therese is white as a cow how.

John Mary submitted to inspection having passed once in a while and being without doubt what they did as answered. And with very much as a joke two saluted as one. John Mary was lonesome James Mary meant to succeed, James Mary in a way James Mary to stay not any longer than John Mary had stayed. John Mary was more than more or less arranged that it should be why. It is very delightful but there is no desire to make preserves until a certain time.

Lucy Church might rest with it as with it as with it with it as an extreme ready to leave it to Felicite. Lucy Church met Lilian Ann St Peter Stanhope to-day and said so. It was a pleasure.

Tie I.

One third.

It occurred to me to add one to three. One to three and afterwards two to three and next three to three. In this way there will be none partly but all wholly.

Would he like to have some of it it is made of it with them. Would he like to have some of it. He has some of it.

It is very necessary to plan.

Lucy Church which when opposite and from a distance then inundated then dated then Lucy Church which when which inundated when which when which

is not a two or more then then when an island can be made by water.

An in day and day and day too to-day and in a day a day a day with poplars where everywhere everywhere identically.

Lucy Church may be that a church may be may be a judge may be pale with eyes may be may be gentle three may be may be that she is a very good very good very good very good and asking if asked would it be theirs and there it is said there there he said that she would she had if it had been given so that in that green and ribbon and if must it is it as it with and lower there may be grown the food that is given not as food but as bedding.

She might she having a little crape in her hair was there. She might having been owning a share was there. She might she might without a doubt she might without a doubt not care if all of them had not thought as well of distributing half when it is not as much as well.

Supposing she liked food. Supposing she knew that it was good would she be younger than thirteen.

Anybody who has a godmother has a godmother.

Simon Therese is a necessity to those who have have it it with with them them then. So she said and wrote it.

John Mary meant meant it as if it was with them and theirs and barely might and might make an occasion. It is a disappointment to have all in order.

Whose is mine. Whose is mine. Whose is mine.

Whose is mine. Whose is whose is whose is mine is mine, whose is mine whose is mine whose is mine.Whose is mine.

The best way to find a second is to look and then to find it. The best way to find the second is to look and then to find it. The best way to find the second is to look and then to find it. The best way to find the second is to look and then to find it. The best way to find the second is to look and then to find it.

The best way to find the second is to look and then to find it.

If there is a river and it is known that it is filled with water and that the water is flowing faster when there is more water it is very easy to see that more water flows into the river and that the water in the river is running along faster very much faster as there is very much more water in the river.

And then likeness.

It is best for Lucy Church to go to church. It is best for John Mary to be well to do and well placed and then leave and settle. It is best for Simon Therese to be met and in a little while to be met and then with then as an invariable left to be known that in there and by it there is an evidence of their return. They may not return there.

It is best that Lilian Ann St. Peter Stanhope might have been with it and having asked them to sing and plan ask many to have habits and be believed and with it with it as it as it in it it is delightful to be that chance.

In a minute.

When there have been five knitting needles and one of them is lost the one that is lost is the fifth needle and it is found. When there are two knitting needles and one of them is lost it is the second one that is lost and it is found but with some difficulty as the information concerning its possible place the place in which it is to be found is accidentally erroneous as it is not to be found there but it is found accidentally and naturally naturally when it is presumed to be presumed that it has been found there as it was. How seriously do they follow the almanac by they they mean the weather.And so and so.

It is very well to establish that it is not a pleasure to lengthen and it is by this means by this means and one day. If books are porcelain and windows are open and fruit is plentiful when will it be very well done. Done and done. That made me remember Felicite. Felicite could ride across. With whom were they left when their father died when their brother-in-law was satisfied to ask them and when their brother was to be considered first. All there all there is.

Lucy Church may be one of those who were not on this side. She certainly is and very many may be who can say very many very many may be very many may be. A river separates water and so it should. A river separates water and so it should.

A river separates water and so it should.
A river separates water and so it should.
A river separates water and so it should.
A river.
A river separates water and so it should.

CHAPTER VI

If asked does she prefer to grow tobacco or look
at birds she says that she prefers as she chooses to
take the tobacco leaves from the tobacco plant which
at a distance smells like a flower and near to smells
tobacco she would prefer since if there is no hail there
can be no destruction and as there is abundance of
water leaves can get to be too big she prefers when one
large bird is attacked by little birds who fly at it and
force it to come lower and lower as there is only the
wind that keeps it as the wings are extended she says
that she chooses the town where affectionately there
had been said that it was not a little as they had known
it to have contained preparation of milk bread and an
adding of it is very well indeed when it is very well
cooked and so and not to go to go on Wednedsay. She
said she preferred the mushrooms that were red and
grew like matches so they were called. Lucy Church
is admirable when there are more fields where clover
is found and also very late when the days are shorter
not dried.

Lucy Church makes a best part of their being by

chance Marcelle said that she preferred. There is no interdependence between between and in as seen. Paul all Paul all if it is when then that that is true one two and furthermore this is what is it when they ask for them to like the best part of their being asked to be inhabited by the ones who are not there if they decide the part that they will take or is to be sent.

Having turned their to the mountain and having wanted to allow them to place themselves one at a time in it as if there is a difference if when there is a snow-mountain mountains around them whether as in Nantua there is no sun or whether as in Caesarieux there is sun whether as in Armandine there is a river or whether as as Bilignin there is no river.

If all of it is in the last time that they are meant to have hunting which is shooting adding to grassing which is ambitiously further left to them. John Mary John Mary who choose chooses chooses John Mary to come to ask may he do so.

John Mary is in the meant to mount all the way up the hill where his home is.

Lucy Church did not like that she being the original there should be copies and this after she had wanted that she being the original there should be copies. Lucy Church was the one who when she came to ask never came at all never came at all by left and right and so may they be whatever they wish to have them do. Very likely what ever they wish to have them do.

She says she knows what they are but she does not know what they will do.

Lucy Church might be addressed when there are two.

Lucy Church might let it be known gradually that if they could they might and if they did they would and she might remove one after the other every little while. She might be very well informed as they are, she might even be very nearly perfectly acquiescent as they say they may they may be called at once to have been astonished speaking of brothers and nieces. There are no more corals than there were. Coral is not grown it is more than that and how many wonder if Piedmont is a name that means near the water between a bay and an ocean.

Lucy Church heard them say that they liked continuity.

It is more continuous to have clouds than rain snow than rain mist than rain hail than rain rain than rain. It is more continuous to have hawks than rain poplars than rain oxen than rain and floods than rain. It is more continuous to have meadows than rain pinks than rain lilies than rain it is more continuous to have hills than rain turns than rain rivers than rain. And so she says and so she says that in the winter they can learn how many more are there to go here and there. John Mary spoke of military service. He said he had seen Sunday and was not difficult it was not difficult to be able every day to work in a field and plant plant it with what had been at other times whatever they had seen. And so. What is it to him whether if there are partly no should he say so. John Mary

finishes Saturday as he is to stay where they go. They go and very additionally it is when it is theirs as well. John Mary has been very rapidly left to it as an afternoon and by the time they like by the time they like. John Mary was as he was to go and be prepared. John Mary understands letting it be theirs delicately. John Mary might be very much more than once in a while. John Mary said nothing as he went. John Mary with it as it is.

Lucy Church made it partly with it now. If it likes a name and there is every reason why it is a name Lucy Church is a name also John Mary also Simon Therese.

Lucy Church did judge so so well of it that it is easily decided that while waiting they would try and see if closed and surrounded is the same as clover and grass. Is the same as clover and grass is the same as leaving it there is the same as well as that is the same that at the time that it was very nearly only a very little that was made to be left alone with pines. Madame Mont Blanc ceased to have charm when the other was found. The other ceased to have charm when the longest way away was found. Found and around are never a solitary instance so he said. If the wind is from the north and there is a slight haze and the tops of the hills are clear the weather will continue to be favourable for the drying of grass and marshes for the blackening of grapes and blackberries and also for the distressing of Lilian Ann St Peter Stanhope who has hopes of every adjoining property becoming

pleasantly a loss and also not having any delight for light which is the result of most of their intention to be nearly ready to await the collecting of what has been grown and gathered. If it as well to part partly at the time that they have been estranged. Remarkably. She was sweet and good looking and insistant and round about and very clearly once in a while in pain and then they could be met met with their having been left alone to like it. Josephine Yvonne Lucy Helen Mary and Xenobie who is nearly as tall as ever and devoted to being industrious and not idle and so forth. Once in a while they are surrounded by supporters and pleasures of the table and of the garden. The garden not having been planted and being considered as soil only of the third quality produces well but not continuously and so it does not. Lucy Church was sitting and to her surprise meant to have it be more carefully placed than as much as if they were more constantly a delight. Lucy Church made no mistake in deciding that this morning they would go and interchangeably. Lucy Church made it appear more nearly when if there might if they were to be contented. Contented too. It could not stop suddenly.

Was it six or a covered place covered by a building and in the corner in the corner in the corner there is an addition to destruction and so strangers will not be pleased and he and she have said that they will not do what they have not said that they will do. Plan to do.

Lucy Church made it be 150 and if forty five is what is asked he the son who is taller will not be especially anxious to be invited but as he was he was not to go. He did not mean to mean to be left lately. So he said he did not mean to be very much as much as at ten. Very much as much as at ten when.

Lucy Church having arranged whether it is more than is left left and right and so might it if it is more in and on and with and much and felt and chosen beside a lake and leaving it behind. And a wind which is useful as they do.

Once every day to prepare hay. Once every day to prepare hay. Once every day once every day to prepare hay. Once every day once every day to prepare hay.

Once every day to prepare hay. What is a wedding a day a wedding to a wedding to a wedding a day. Lucy Church said that her mother was accustomed to baptism and her mother said that she was accustomed to baptism uniquely accustomed to baptism.

It is after and because of this which is in a reliable and relatively after it is met and with it as alighted from which when it is before it is and left. If after it is with and with it in there there and best of it with a begun and with it as a joining there in time to be in place of which withstand. It is by the left and more of it which made it be theirs in the investigation of ordinarily and as much as it if in and and at at that and at that rate and how. He was left to out of it to out and in and with and by their have it left to two

two two makes which if they are occupied and with at left it might can be and should their heads buried in clover.

Lucy Church their heads buried in clover.

He with a in a case of did he did he leave it with the come to be in coming shall it for this in this can it might it after all when tall tall taller let it be as much as could and chance a chance out right out-right at all. Very quietly.

It is not higher than hats than hats it is not higher than oaks it is not higher than pharmacy it is not higher than held. It is not higher than apples and pears it is not higher than left it to them it is not higher than if they wish it is not higher than with it with it with it as much as much as as will as with it. Lucy Church could know that they had gone there as they did and if told it would have interested her as everything that they did interested her and what they did habitually and they habitually did what is what they did interested her and she was interested when she was told what they did.

She was she was she was to leave to leave to have to have to have to have have have this have this have this.

John Mary asked if the weather had been oppressive.

Simon Therese was to meet Edith.

Lilian Ann St Peter Stanhope might be accounted as having heard two.

Jenny Church has found it and has been told that

it has been found by a neighbour and she was confused and did not attend to it so she says. All of them are uncertain when there is to be ceremony ceremony is occasioned by religion and by separation.

John Mary entitles entitled entices them to be and come to be to remain.

James Mary is an element in their having three come to be when one two three.

Lucy Church in once and poised. There is a difference in having asked why do once do once do once do do face it. This makes it do do what is a crow a magpie a hawk to do if five little birds attack one big one. What are they to do a magpie a hawk a crow to do. What is it that they do what is it that they are to do.

Lucy Church made a road wind in the distance and it is known to be a road by a culvert which keeps it from being washed away by water which can be poured upon it as rain or as trickling.

With and without in the distance there is much about is it to be sure that it is as if flour is made by their giving and their getting and if it were to be for them they if he did not like it would leave her to see to it, so she said.

Lucy Church would decide that it was best beside sunset in the afternoon which it does everywhere as they share they place and they place it there there where like it like it like it like it like it a stream of she was looking to see and she saw she said she saw she would be very much better pleased if all mushrooms

were edible and she said she liked to have it known very well known very well it is merely by this that that that is that it is with that that it is it is if they asked which are the best the best or readily dividing green from seen it is what they might do to ask if five are offered and four are taken what is the difference between five and four. Five and no more five and four four and four four or five five or five or four. In this way a bank a bank of a stream a stream of a sun a sun of a shade a shade of a lawn a lawn of clover and very five feet five feet makes it demonstrable that to copy it a little more and play play it for them. Never stopping doing this to do that.

It is very well to take it as a coral necklace and turn to take it as a coral necklace and turn to take it as a coral necklace and turn and if white and wool makes silk what is it that is in the field. What is it that is in the field oxen and son and some and very much more attached to them now. They are very much more attached to them now. How and now. He having told Lilian Ann St Peter Stanhope that she is coming to be in and out and about and how about it. If they do not feel it how do they know that it is ready to put away. In moving it they can tell and as it is better for it to keep it in motion there is no difficulty in knowing when it is ready to be put away. This they do not say as no one asks them as it has been done and a taller one is curving with a smaller one and neither of them is curving.

Lucy Church can stay and see how happily she can

stay and see and be where she can be and stay and see and presumably she can see and stay and see presumably it is always doubtful if they will go and to what distance and once or twice. It is a very serious matter to count poplars.

Lucy Church wishes that it has been as much and as often as there has been an answer. Answer and answers.

Lucy Church with when then slowly and very often left alone. Left alone with an arrangement of five two in back one in front and below a river. So she says.

It has to do with through.

Then why they will it is will it will it will it will it be will it be waste wasted will it be wasted. Baskets which are not in use are with this with this with this and Yenne. Yenne is an available place for the place places where where if as if as in little to be shown shown and seen set and settle weather settle it is a very great difference north and south if known and she as much as said they were to lay it there presumably. Lucy Church counted five.

Lucy Church in reunion. If he had been asked to give it not to give it but to receive to give it and to receive a hand which should be ready to receive it and to give it if he should have been ready and it was left as it was whose is as much as if they knew they knew though through poplars into trees though hills into wills through whether into weather through theirs and this into where there is that which is as if it might be

Lucy Church and she had it she had not been made to be left to it in September Lucy Church may be.

There is no difference between discomfort and uncomfortable. When a tree looks to be that it would with difficulty be laid upon the ground two of them are taken and one of them being left it is when it is seen that they are able to have them offer a young girl.

Neither John Mary nor James Mary have liked and made the best of it with eight and yellow and dandelions which being of a colour are neither mauve nor orange.

John Mary need not have to go and stay and he need not prefer having met many expectedly. He need not leave it as if they were mainly attracting this to that. It is very nicely that he may.

Lucy Church means fuschias because fuschias grow in pots and have very pretty baskets very pretty paper and sewing very pretty rose and purple very pretty leaves and heights very pretty here to Lucy very pretty Lucy Pagoda very pretty when then seen growing as if vines in colour growing where they make it appear Lucy Church Pagoda. Lucy Church Pagoda Lucy Church Lucy Church Lucy.

John Mary knows that if it snows John Mary with and widen John Mary to be led to stay and stand and a bell a bell can tell that eels are in water and no farther. Fresh water eels are delicious if fresh water eels are delicious.

Thomas Mary and for awhile James Mary and for

that as in time to be sure. If all day and all night is a mistake how many have they had to choose. To choose.

Lucy Church made heaven a hand. Lucy Church and come to be glad that three times are very much with them that they are there. Lucy Church with them. That they are there.

Simon Therese answers and was more than it could with this as when two and two they might two and two there it was and in with very when and opposition. Sometimes they make cake better there than there.

Simon Therese face to face face to face literally and face to face literally it is in between that they have made it be that if that and that and.

John Mary close to carry John Mary leaves it out without meaning that in that one alone three are married this means that they have been poor and in poverty letting it be like and liking they keep their where there. And so it is when they die.

There are more in as intended in and with it could oranges grow on a mountain they can they do when the snow does not lie and they are inside unheated and many weddings are in winter and waited. It is very likely that windows are windows in here. Very likely.

Lucy Church propaganda Lucy propaganda Lucy Church propaganda Lucy Church propaganda Lucy Lucy Church Lucy Church propaganda Lucy propaganda Lucy Church propaganda.

Hours of hours of having seen in between between

vines express to white and there and if a river is water then having it as access it might Lucy it might Lucy Church and Pagoda.

It might Lucy Lucy Church Lucy Church Lucy Church and Pagoda. Lucy Church intermediary intermediary between at a distance in between and though through with through with when Yenne through with through. Lucy Church Pagoda understood.

Simon Therese made Simon Therese mountains of in case Simon Therese in place in place of Simon Therese in case Simon Therese felt in Simon Therese in case Simon Simon Therese in place Simon Therese lace. Simon Therese. Simon Therese meant absent. Simon Therese as place Simon Therese in case Simon Therese Simon Therese very willow will will well. It is very often that a very large willow and any willow will grow in a marsh where sometimes the grass is burned and sometimes it is not. A willow will sometimes split in two. John Mary because of John Mary James Mary to succeed John Mary when John goes away to marry. He is to marry Mary so it is said. Sometimes they do not marry and sometimes they do marry. Sometimes they do marry.

Lucy Church is as is as it is intended as it is as it is to suggest. She is going away and she says that in any case it is useful.

Lilian Anne St Peter Stanhope may make rain if it is when it is as stronger it is very as much stronger as theirs to place. Did she sleep eleven hours or longer.

CHAPTER VII

Pansy Died and Pansy Lewis are not introduced.
In affection.

Pansy Lewis was named after a flower as was her
sister Rose Lewis and her sister Lily Lewis. Her two
brothers were named Robert Lewis and George Lewis.
They were all of them very much better acquainted
with left and right and very much as if it had been that
there was more than if after it had been once they had
left it to them.

Lucy Church add added that a very large house
was built with small rooms. This was because it had
been built one hundred years ago and even so.

Lucy Church was with a name and Lucy Church
and with a name a name and allowed. Peaches are
yellow or crimson and apples are green or red and pears
hang like pears and then it is said said of them that
there is more fruit than there was but not more in
addition.

Very well I thank you and as to a cloud they say it
is on the mountain but a mountain is not a mountain
if there is pasture to repeat that a mountain is not a

mountain if there is pasture. To repeat that a mountain is not a mountain if there is a mountain which has
a pasture on it, which has pasture on it.

Lucy Church made many many many come to be
to stay and stand and having said Lamartine all is said.

Having said Lamartine all is said in respect to the
best direction to be given to be comfortably left to
heaven. Comfortably left. To heaven. Lamartine
and questioning, now there has been a change even
within three years there has been a change within
three years there has been a change now they do not
begin with them there has been this change within
these three years there has been this change.

Lucy Church made her sister be named Frances
Church, the sister was older and had been named Frances
Church. She was prepared to be here and she was
here and this was a comfort and might be very well
and easily pleased. Lucy Church was seen in the
distance between two hills and not a long distance from
Yenne but slightly higher and could be easily seen to
be Lucy Church Lucy Church Pagoda and it is with
some difficulty that not being remembered Lucy
Pagoda could be confounded with Yvonne Pagoda at
one time. Yvonne Pagoda being forgotten could be
remembered with difficulty until if it happened that
they were there it would be very charming to see
Yvonne Pagoda stand and not pass and surrounded
and surrounded and surrounded as much as is indeed
with it at a distance. Yvonne Pagoda is her name.
Just the same.

Lucy Church in intention.

John Mary meant it to be that Paul is the one who with this difference is very much to be added to younger. John Mary has been held to have to be left to be known that his brother James Mary is to succeed later succeed later and Lucy Church may not be there.

Simon Therese and Lilian Ann St Peter Stanhope cannot be led and said. Said so said so and there is no statue younger than the statue of Lamartine. She saw it said. And one and said.

Simon Therese and own.

Lucy Church was as was one and one. Lucy Church made it be that she was anxious to see that the three which were there could be reached one after the other if there was one after the other if there is one after the other they can be reached as there are the three there one to the right one to the left and one in the middle and two of them can be reached one one of them can be reached from the right and two of them can be reached from the right and two of them can be reached from the middle.

Lucy Church can not be seen from there.

John Mary and the contents of the basket John Mary and the slowness of the separation of the division of it all into the basket. John Mary and the preparation of the most that has been shown to be left to it for the preparation in their and left and right entirely entirely left to it that it was not as much as if this is when there is when and what and by the blissful and eradicated allowing it to close. John Mary is allowing it to ·be

their choice and if it is not notably notably and nobly nobly and with it well with it John Mary met and meant and with it if three leave and two come none are here.   This is with as if a light rose mauve makes lilies in green grass.   John Mary made a distant right and left and if after rose if after all if after Dolly if after rose if after rose if after all if after well if after with it as and Ida with it as and as and with it as with with it it is by the sound the rain.   John Mary John Mary with with with it as if in it they were cut out with the same and there was to cover and there was to cover and there was to cover it a globe so called just the same.   John Mary likes the attention.

Lucy Church prefers the sun to the rain but finds both monotonous she prefers a temperate climate where the snow does not stay upon the ground where the mountains are poetical the rivers wide and rapidly flowing the meadows green and the poplars very tall and the newly planted ones very thin and pretty and delicate.   She also likes the people to be nearly as well to do as they are and to live in the enjoyment of butter cake nut oil and fowl and also to find many of the natural growths to be pale yellow mauve blue and purple and rose and very miniature also the sun flowers to be planted if they are useful.   She also wishes it to be understood that a pagoda combined with a church is something but a pagoda in stone and not combined with a church is something else.   She has plenty of time to arrange everything and she has been asked to like it very much.

Simon Therese is not announced and with it and called called Simon Therese Thursday. Thursday there is present Lilian Anne St Peter Stanhope and she is aroused by their reunion and very naturally allowed. There are very many to spare and with it as they might sojourn and research and plan and plunder and isolate and depend and identify and necessitate and withdraw and very hastily light candles if there has been a disappearance of the ordinary fuel which is what is an illuminant and so they please them.

Simon Therese with it as would they carry.

Simon Therese more and more it is not necessary that they are idolised. Simon Therese more and more it is with them that they saw that there is finally a very new place to be seen which not having been used is to be used and is to be green. A meadow is to be green. A meadow is to be green. It is to be used as pasture as clover as a road and as a better send her. It is also theirs to be wish. Simon Therese might be at the time that there is a profession which is a difference between a procession and a thing to be seen between and between. Simon Therese can change his mind.

John Mary with it as if Mary which is Xenobie never could be left handed and left and right said that it is best that if it is to be tried she she knew that it was best to stay and every year four coming from there were to be arranging that they were to receive who came. Delightful.

CHAPTER VIII

Was Lucy Church pleased she was very pleased with the difference between here and there. There there is a lake here there is a lake. There there is a garden and woods and trees and here here there is a garden and woods and trees. Here there are meadows and a moon. There there are not meadows and there is a moon. Here there are lights and trees there there are lights and trees. Here there are sounds due to marshes there there are sometimes sounds due to marshes. There is this there. There there is this there and so there is. Lucy Church is very pleased. It is with it as with it. If it is placed there it is not worth while. If it is not it is placed in another place and Lucy Church does put it there. Lucy Church finds it satisfactory not only that it shall be as large and as round as it is but also that it is successfully put it where when it is to be accepted it will be immeasurably placed. Lucy Church might wish for everything. John Mary would find it admirable to leave it every day exactly might find it admirable to leave it every day exactly. John Mary with it can have will come to be classing classing an arch an arch which can say

come to-day in an arch which can say to come to-day
and so it is within because any one asking it of him is
certain to be asked to be asked to be asked as it is
nearly with it as with it as with it as it is best. Best
and most. Simon Therese understands winning that
is to say inventing winning Simon Therese that
is to say Simon Therese that is to say understands
inventing winning Simon Therese that is to say
understands inventing winning. Simon Therese that is
to say understands inventing winning.

That is to say it develops very well.

Simon Therese that is to understands inventing
winning that is to say it develops very well that is to
say Simon Therese that is to say understands inventing
winning that is to say it develops very well.

A place with it as an intention to leave it as it is
best to be shown with when if and made it be may be
may like which it is not only that before with and
might come as in contrast in between it is more than
is most with it partially with for instance and hand
and at hand and in a hand and with it could a lake be
larger and with it to change it to and if to if to and to
and to and to to be fair. Put it there. Lucy Church
likes mauve lilies that grow freely.

Simon Therese with it and sparingly and fortunately fortunately as there are groups under the trees
and fortunately as there are groups under the trees
and they do partially prepare what they share partially
prepare what they share Simon Therese to care Simon
Therese with care Simon Therese partly Simon The-

rese partly would it be well to remind that it cannot
be placed there him that it cannot be placed there.
John Mary with their devotion to Josephine and to
wedding wedding in a pleasure of recognising porcelain
in swimming pleasure in recognising that they are circling what is circling in a half circle mushrooms are
circling in a half circle and they are matches and are
so cold pleasing so called pleasing to the palate and
pleasing so called half a circle so called very largely so
called so called meadows as they are very nearly higher
than a mountain a marsh or anything. Anything is
best for them. Lucy Church is not more than if she
were gone gone again as they made it do so do so do
that do that do that too. Too can be arranged and
very well I thank you. She was if it is made to-day.
If it is made to-day. He could go where they went
very easily.

Milly Lamartine I mean, I mean I mean or am I
mistaken is it two places.

There are as a little with it as at once as is it as it
is and is it as is it as at once. Very little as at once as
it is as is it as is it as it is as is it as at once. Very little
as it is as it is as is it as at once.

It would take very little to make it as it is as it is
as it is to prepare and to deny that that with and by
if it can leave mind and mind it and wind winding a
string which has not been too long and adding a whole
one. This can make any one long for Madeleine Madeleine who is freely succeeded by their following me.
When this you see acceptably and with it as if with

her with it as if with her Madeleine Lucy Church Celestine
Lucy Church Susy Lucy Church Mary Lucy Church.
Lucy Church which one imagine which one. Which
one Lucy Church which one imagine which one and
not neglected no not neglected imagine which one Lucy
Church no not neglected imagine which one.

Lucy Church might find Mary Lucy Church
gradually adding Mary Lucy Church gradually adding
which one Mary Lucy Church gradually adding. Lucy
Church gradually adding Lucy Church which one Lucy
Church gradually Lucy Church which one. Madeleine
Lucy Church gradually Lucy Church gradually Lucy
Church gradually gradually adding which one. Madeleine Lucy Church which one gradually adding Madeleine Lucy Church gradually adding Madeleine Lucy
Church which one Lucy Church gradually gradually
adding which one.

John Mary is authorized to explain parts of their
pitcher parts of their pitcher which contains very good
milk very good flour very pretty flowers very good
honey and very good water. John Mary is authorized
to explain that a very good pitcher contains very
good water very good flour very good honey very good
milk and very pretty flowers. John Mary is authorized
to explain that a very good pitcher contains very
good flour very good water very good honey very good
milk and very pretty flowers.

John Mary is authorized to explain that they have
everything there exactly as they had John Mary is
authorized to explain that they have everything there

that they had there when it was just as well that they had everything there when they had it there. John Mary was authorized to explain that in the midst of mountains there is no in the midst of mountains because there is a place that is very agreeable where they are. John Mary is authorized to explain that at least at first they have had it as if it were that they would go and make it be as if they were to be to like it at all. John Mary was authorized is authorized to have and let it be what is at once or twice and by the way and feel it as it is. John Mary is authorized to need to be not to need to need not to be with it where they have it come. It is in the country in a country where they speak of it that it is known.

Simon Therese comes to leave Simon Therese comes to leave comes to leave comes to leave and with it very sombrely comes to leave and with it comes to leave and with it comes to leave. He could have known when. When was it.

It is of no importance to introduce them whether whether they are there, whether they are whether they are whether they are whether they are there altogether whether they are altogether there. It is of no importance to introduce them altogether whether they are there.

She likes very much what has been given to her.

CHAPTER IX

John Mary has a brother James Mary and James Mary has just been in Morocco and now he is here. There are quite a number who are here who have been in Morocco. James Mary is to remain here. James Mary is six or seven or seven or six years younger than his brother John Mary. There are other John Marys in the town one of them is several years older and has been called and has turned and has entered into conversation but the conversation is not of long duration.

John Mary finding a hill-side to be covered with vines and wheat and not very good potatoes is content that his father was not aided as his father was very much more than his mother not aided. This has not been a grief to more than marching not been a grief to more than marching. John Mary can always not be divided between the two statues one to a dead defender and the other to a dead provider and so a fife is a fife and five drummers are five drummers and it is as much as it is well to be kept three. Three and then seven and ten twenty-four and beside and sixty-two and very much very much as if it were left to be alone.

John Mary not having much grass has to borrow beasts horned beasts and now he owns three three at a time and very well I thank you.

John Mary has never explained having left it to them he has never explained having left it to them and he has never explained having left it to them. Bertha has never explained having left it to them. Bertha is the name of Bertha as if it were used and as if it were used. Bertha is the name of Bertha as if it were used and it is not admirable as if it were used it all depends upon it being done again as if it were used as if it were used. Astonishingly as if it were used. If it were used. Come and if it were used. As if it were used. Bertha astonishingly as if it were used. If it were used. As if it were used.

Association and disassociation as if it were used one two three as if it were used four six eight as if it were used five four three as if it were used one two three as if it were used.

John Mary would have been left to that and if he had a Spanish fever he would have died. He had a Spanish fever but it was later not very much later one year later and if he had had the Spanish fever he would have died. John Mary understands loss he understands exactitude he understands gentleness he understands placing he understands willows he understands attending he understands undeniable he understands their having it as much as that he understands having been to the burial of an older man whom he has known. John Mary likes to have been very well. He is very well.

John Mary might made and candles candles supplant electricity when electricity goes out but does it. John Mary was remembered because milk is milk and brother is brother and vines are vines and wheat can be compared to wheat by him he compares it. And so to be so to be so very so very soon so very soon as so very soon as well. John Mary might try.

John Mary and John Mary and James Mary and James Mary one and one make two.

Lucy Church is entirely different she is entirely different from Madeleine Church entirely different from Jessie Church entirely different and not withstanding they can arrange entirely different and not withstanding. Let it be known as theirs alone and so and so to have it go.

CHAPTER XI

They have left they who have been out all night have left they have left they who have left have come back again that is some of them. They have come back again some of them they have left all of them they have come back again some of them those of them who were wanted that is wanted that is were wanted. John was surprised and he was not with them but he went and he met them and he was not surprised and they went on going going to where there was not a wedding but a celebrating of there having been Brillat Savarin. It sounds so but it was so. They went on down to where they could not get in all of them they could get in all of them only women all of them could get in they did get in all of them got in. Therese who had not been wishing was inviting and the morning in the morning they came out of having been gone as they were gone they were not there they were gone and they were all delaying not all delaying and not at all in a minute delaying and they were all there as in a minute delaying. Then they were foolish to have been.

Lucy Church and her sister Frances Church and her mother and her brother she did not have a brother it is Helen who had a brother and three sisters and a father Lucy Church had two sisters and a father and a mother and of her it was said not Lucy. And of her it was said not Lucy it was said of her not Lucy. Lucy had been not confused but having two weeks before admitted that John could and did and it was of no interest to any one as it was so much worse and had often been remarked upon by any one even he he knew it not John but one of whom nobody said anything that is to say of whom every one said not only but also as it is at once. Very well I thank you. It is as good. Very well I thank you.

Lucy Church might and right right and left left and right and might. Might it.

Very nice and quiet I thank you.

It is very delightful that they could see and so that they could see and so they could see and so that they could see and so. That they could see that they could see and so. It is very delightful that they could see and so they could see they could see and so it is very delightful that they could see. It is very delightful that they could see and so.

There is no difference between here and there and there and there is a difference between if it is I mean. I mean. There is no difference between here and there between I mean I mean. Every time to see a green tree turn yellow and we did not. Every time and we did not to see a green tree to see it turn yellow and we

did not. Why did we not because on account not only
on account but we could not have anticipated that we
left early this year.

Lucy Church made it at once having Lucy Church
made it at once having Lucy Church made it at once
having. Having left across not having left across and
now having entered into a period of being higher than
ever it has been sold it has been sold valuably.

All along.

Lucy Church. Having had. Never needing. Once
or twice. If more. Three or five. Three kinds.
One one two two three three and one of them even two
of them could be were and can be erased.

Introducing Albert Bigelow who was of course
Albert Bigelow know the ending of ending Albert Bigelow can not know know William Mary who was first
a boy then an and and then and and then and and
then and he has been adding adding a million to three
which makes a million and three and this was sent
sent away to accomplish every day every day. Albert
Bigelow know William Mary. Albert Bigelow know
William Mary. William Mary. Albert Bigelow know
William Mary.

Albert Bigelow come to know that his sister his
sister and he made made and missed missed and missed
her. Albert Bigelow did not come alone he had hur-
ried to come and go Albert Bigelow to say so oh to say
so oh to say so Albert Bigelow.

Albert Bigelow had not known Lucy Church nor
John Mary nor Simon Therese. John Mary did not

know William Mary nor Albert Bigelow nor would he. Why should he. He might if it were not that they were not at all yesterday or to-day to be any day anywhere except there. Thank you so much. Very nice and quiet I thank you.

One two one two all out but you all out but you three four three four shut the door shut the door five six five six they will be best best and most most and best namely, Lucy Church John Mary and Simon Therese who do not know why they like to show that it is a very beautiful country and it has been left to be regained that is to say honey is attractive when it is made of accacia cake is attractive when it is made of Caesar and Caesarness and poplars are attractive when a great many are poplars are attractive. Never come to be Albert Bigelow never, come, to, be, Albert Bigelow. Never come to be Albert Bigelow Albert Bigelow has said that he is added and in added. William Mary is not partly at one time. Two at one time John Mary and James Mary John Mary is to marry Mary Crane who is a very attractive woman although frequently ill. Together they will work hard. It is the habit of the country to do so so it is the habit of the country to do so. Very well I thank you.

Lucy Church and Lucy Pagoda comparably.

Albert Bigelow meet William Mary. John Mary meet William Mary.

William Mary meet Albert Bigelow.

William Mary marry and be very well to do.

William Mary meet Albert Bigelow and find it used to
be used to it.

John Mary meet William Mary.   It was not needed.
That is to say William Mary in travelling it was not
needed.   William Mary married and was very well
to do and had a villa in Saint Cloud where he was very
well to do and pleasantly.

John Mary was not understood to have his attention drawn to him as in the summer in the course of
the summer he was very much occupied with his prepara-
tions and with his activities and with his arrangements
and very quietly and very quietly smiling if he he was
called and came called and came.   Very well I thank
you.   He was to be very much appreciated and to
be succeeded by his brother James Mary.   Yes he
was and just about now.   Yes he was and just about
now.

Simon Therese and just about now.   Lilian Anne
St Peter Stanhope and just about just just about
now just about.

Simon Therese added attractively to just about
now.   Simon Therese added, to, attractively just
about now.   Simon Therese added just attractively
just about now.   Simon Therese just attractively
added about now attractively just about attractively
added just about now.

To knew to know just about how to knew to now
just about how.   Attractively just about now.   To
knew to know just about just about how just about
now to knew to know to know to knew attractively

added to just about now. Added attractively how
just about how just about now added attractively.

Knew added attractively knew just about now
how how attractively knew attractively added knew
attractively just about about now. Simon Therese
added attractively just about now. Simon Therese
just about how. They were very silent when intend
intend to send send Albert Bigelow to Lilian Stanhope
and ask her to be sure to have it as it is what is meant
by very pleasantly and very quietly and very
confusedly and very much as it was with it books in
porcelain and birds in butter. Birds in butter may be
mistaken for birds in potatoe and neither do much
harm. If they are white they are pleasant to the eye.

Could it be winding up and down directly with it
as if it were that there was a bird on top and on top
and in and on the side and very much which if it is as
added as that by the way by the way in a custom and
in a custom custom custom custom and funny it is very
much as much as honey honey perfumed by accacia and
having a substance is delectable.

To look to see and to see that as it is that bread
and that it is that it is with a way to be in and as much
as they can see to say. Having come she would look
like that so they say. Lucy Church having come she
would look like that and if she were to be seen she
would if she were to mean to be seen to be seen she
would be busy. She would look like that it is as much
as if as much as like that. It is as much in as much
for as much with as much as as much as if as much as

it is with it in the most of it that it is very little as alike and there is a difference between red at night is a sailors delight and red in the morning is a sailors warning and poplars trees which now might turn a little yellow if they see if they see see the green which is used in between. It might be grown grass. It is only necessary to be known to be grown that there they have it to spare three times every year and need to have it burn if it is soaked by an inundation. Very like it is if in standing he has been walking and very well and to be said to be expecting it as much as any day partly with them. And if it is Simon Therese if it is Simon Simon Therese has been in.

Simon Therese has a mother who has been well and Simon Therese and Simon Therese has a mother who has been well.

Janet Church has had a sister and she is very well and very well is better than before.

John Mary has a mother and a father and the father has been well but is not so well has been as well his father has been as well the father of John Mary and the mother of John Mary have been very strong and very well.

Chrysanthemums ordinary ones are different from cactuses which are not those that have not been crossed with lilies. Very well I thank you. Prepare it very well very well I thank you. Very nice and quiet I thank you prepare it I thank you very well I thank you very well very nice and very nice and very nice and very quiet very nice very well very well I thank you.

Simon Therese as a place.

Simon Simon Therese will he will he could Edith be a name could Lucy be a name could Alice be a name could Eugenia be a name could Dorothy be a name could Victoria be a name. Simon Therese had made wide and wide and around and perhaps and a stair. He was one of them.

William Mary suitable to William and Mary.

Lucy Church far away to say that that having rested they could do it now. Having been asked are there more sisters than brothers she would say you can tell yes.

Lucy Church you can tell yes and yes. Yes and yes. You can tell less and less you can tell yes and yes. Lucy Church Lucy and Church Lucy and Lucy Lucy and Lucy Church. Whom might be very well as very well yesterday to-day and now. Lucy Church might have been rain. Lucy Church might have been going and hearing in the rain. It is not difficult to hear in the rain because it is slippery that is it is not slippery nor is it muddy it is watery.

Lucy Church did not sing it is not the habit of the country to sing.

Lucy Church did and did not go it is not the habit of the country not to go not to stay not to go and stay and stay and go. It is not the habit of the country not a habit of the country to stay not the habit of the country to stay not to go not the habit of the country not to go. Lucy Church could have changed she could say he did as well as that and it was a mistake because

it showed that having become older she was older than younger that is to say younger. Displeasing not displeasing not displeasing arouse not displeasing arouse not displeasing arouse not displeasing arouse displeasing not displeasing.

Neither Lucy Church nor John Mary are interested. Simon Therese is interested.

Those who do not know that to say so is this. Please pay pray and relieve which is might and butter with it ordered as before near a station a station can be known as a depot it can be known as fruit and a fruiterer it can be known as for and before and before and for before. It can and can and can be be known as known as before.

If with and add.

Never have a half to be a half to be a half to be to be to be a half a half a half a half to be.

Thanks to be.

Lucy Church may be left to be thanks to be.

Lucy Church thanks to be.

Lucy Church thanks to be.

Lucy Church if if it were after it after it if it if and after after if it thanks to be.

Lucy Church thanks.

Lucy Church found it desirable to have it better intended if indeed they in the and intending if in the in the intending and liking likewise made to be they were expecting Simon. Simon Therese is not the same as if a pearl as if a pearl were pale and if a pearl were pale very pale irritably she she might be coming

back this evening and very pleased with meeting her mother and meeting her father and greeting her father her mother her mother and her father. It is understood that when they leave it they leave the country for the city. It is understood when they leave it they leave the city for the country. It is understood when they leave it they do not leave it alone they do not leave it alone because they like it they do not leave it alone because there are very many there they do not leave it alone because they add left to right left left left right left thank you.

It is not known that Lucy Church abandoned it entirely. It is not known that very little further there is no difference between very little further. It is not known that as it is Minnie Minnie Rate they might as well state how many very much as much as there are as many how many there are are is added to delicately they might install in vain. Thank you very much and please be quiet. Thank you very much as much as ever. Thank you.

Lucy Church with with withstand Lucy Church with with with withstand Lucy Church it might have it that they were enjoying it.

Lucy Church with withstand.

Lucy Church with withstand Lucy Church with Lucy Church with withstand.

Lucy Church rented a valuable house for what it was worth. She was prepared to indulge herself in this pleasure and did so. She was not able to take possession at once as it was at the time occupied by a

lieutenant in the french navy who was not able to make
other arrangements and as the owner of the house was
unwilling to disturb one who in his way had been able
to be devoted to the land which had given birth and
pleasure to them both there inevitably was and would
be delay in the enjoyment of the very pleasant situation which occupying the house so well adapted to the
pleasures of agreeableness and delicacy would undoubtedly continue. And so it was.

Lucy Church might be if as planned. And very
much in attending to finding anything at once agreeable and if there was continuity an indifferently variably fatigue and so forth with them in exchange. It
is not an indifference which makes them give themselves pleasure not at all not at all an attentiveness
that makes them give themselves pleasure not at all
and not at all. It was by and by as if and to wonder
is the river as a river as a river as a better and better
and wider and wider and very much as much smaller
as if allowed allowed to be sure surely it is not partly
they they are replaced by once more than at all with
likely very much and very and likely to be nearly
with when and letting letting theirs be nearly, it is nicely left to which one and which one is it.

Lucy Church immoderately and Lucy Lucy how
many how many weeks how many weeks are there in
September and November how many weeks are there
in September and how many weeks are there to be to
make the whole of November. She was very pleased
to answer. Every answer turns away wrath. So it does.

Lucy Church did not like to see roses open too quickly because that would mean that tube roses would not completely open. Do understand that. Lucy Church did not like Lucy Church did not like that Lucy Church did not like that roses should open too quickly because that would mean that tube-roses would not open completely.

Lucy Church is in one and two. Lucy Church is in.

Lucy Church and to be sure to be certain to be certainly to be certainly.

Lucy Church may be any one. How many are there who are left by it. Lucy Church she knows. She is mistaken in thinking that he could have done it as well really mistaken.

It is easy to avoid so Lucy should have known it is easy to avoid having been engulfed by their being just as well as ever easy to avoid having been leading in more than it is more than it is partly that. Lucy Church should be forgotten. Frances Church should be there. Mr. and Mrs. Church might be might be and very prettily there is a difference between prettily and happily. There is a difference between happily and audibly there is a difference between waiting and calling. Thank you so much. Very well I thank you thank you so, much.

CHAPTER XII

It might be that Simon Therese was fifty two forty two thirty two twenty and twenty-one times five. How do you do.

CHAPTER XIII

She liked to know that he loved her so and apart
from adding how many. Lucy Church could be and
mutton mutton mutton and button button button and
mutton Lucy Church and he loved her so and with it
fresh from a statue of a mathematician set in trees
which when there is fruit near them makes a very little
cactus prefer porcelain to silver. Silver to silver and
after all very nice and quiet I thank you.

Lucy Church was very near adding was very near
adding a pagoda to a center of irradiation of there being
and belonging Kates and pleasing and please be with
this with this. Think very well of their adding think
very well of their sleeping think very well of in a minute think very well Lucy Church may be made and may
be and with it in it with it with it with it with it who
has who has had whom who has who has as quickly who
has as slowly said said it and be why could could made
made with it in a doubtful should it be their share.
Lucy Church knows the difference in a circumstance.

One two three four five six Katherine and Albert
both of them thin and win then and won there and

where this and lie lie on the table and say how often does it all need what they say. Be very careful of sitting near the fire as it is very likely to make one desire to have four of them need everything four of them need everything to-day as they like what they have to leave once or twice for and before before which is with them with them makes it taught as much as if they had asked how often do they additionally please and forgetting what it was that she said. She said I like it.

Simon Therese in does it win.

Simon Therese in. In it. Simon Therese with all of it as they must be must it be must it be that they like Simon Therese must must be that they like.

John Mary never can state close. Close it. John Mary away from winning it as if they might prefer going up and down and do prefer going up and down do prefer, going up and down. Do prefer going up and down.

CHAPTER XIV

Who made it ask it with it is it is it for it let it can it can it.

Can it be as much as if they like it forever.

Forever comes to be more capable of its being left alone to like widen widen popularly left to them because of it having had it as with it presently coming to have more than they had in contrast. In contrast.

Lucy Church in meadows and very well remembering and very well remembering Lily Lilian very well remembering mauve lilies with a short stem. Stems are shorter than after all in adaptably placed in partly an opening of in and irreplaceable their way. It was part of the time. Theirs with them too. Gradually remembering a lake. Gradually. Remembering. A lake. In gradually remembering a lake by the shore of the lake where they were sitting. In gradually remembering they were eating not this time they remembered with it and settling settling relating relation to what is more there than fancy. Fancy a bee sitting and never to be dangerous to any one. Katherine a particle and love and lose Katherine a particle and Katherine a

particle love and lose Katherine a particle. And with
it who made who made them like like it. Like it.

Lucy Church need not change the number of days
in which it is very necessary that she should ask them
how do they account for it.

Simon Church could be the name of any one named.
Named nomenclature passively plainly paying this for
them and as much as when they could. Could count
it.

Lucy Church who has been able to preserve cake
freshly for three months. Lucy Church and her
mother and this not because of any talent on the part
of Lucy Church but because of the material the
country affords. They are all equally favoured.

Simon Therese is a very sad spectacle. He is no
longer as he was and this may be not his fault but very
likely he will never again make it a pleasure never again
never altogether and Simon Therese altogether he and
altogether was and altogether is and altogether.
Simon Therese altogether is and was and they are
this is altogether Simon Therese is and is altogether.
Altogether to be said.

Simon Therese comes to Edith Edith comes to Simon
Therese separately. Simon Therese separately.

Simon Therese is with it Simon Therese and purse
Simon Therese and this Simon Therese and very with
them very with them very very with with them. This
is not what what with with it. It is a moon Sunday
and Monday it is a moon Monday. It is a moon Monday it is a sun Sunday it is a sun Monday it is a moon

Sunday.   It is a moon Monday.   It is a moon Sunday.
It is a sun Monday.   It is a sun Thursday.   It is a sun
Wednesday.   It is a sun Sunday.   It is a sun Monday.
Simon Therese it is a sun Monday.

Simon Therese has plenty of place.

It is very well to wish.

It is very well to wish on me.

It is very well to wish on me.

It is very well to wish it is very well to wish on me.

It is very well to wish on me.

CHAPTER XV

He got up and he sat down and he walked around. He came back. He liked it. He was ready to tell her what she should tell him. He hesitated. He was very much obliged. He was as much as you like what is as much as you like. He was called William Mary and he employed Albert Bigelow. As William Mary he lived here. As employing Albert Bigelow he lived here. As getting up sitting down and walking around he lived here. Little by little he lived here. He was after all after a while after once in a while he was very well I thank you. William Mary as might be remarked had been in Belley but only a day and it was the visit was of no importance. William Mary I thank you. Very well I thank you.

William Mary occasionally, William Mary and his wife older and his wife older. This is with with this. Thank you very much.

That is as if she had brought a complete set of ink blotters paper holders and everything from Florence for him. Thank you.

One two three thank you. One two three one two three one two three thank you.

One two three he would please me. Please me.

John Mary could not be remembered to me. He could not be remembered to me and William Mary could not be remembered to me. William Mary could not be remembered to me.

Why do false heliotropes smell strongly of heliotrope because they look as if they were more hardy. William Mary does not live in the same country as William Tell and that is because there is a frontier between. This gives rise to the opinion that in between there is more than ever one lake one lake gives rise to the impression that as there is nobody at present to interfere there is no difference at all between a church and a pagoda no difference at all between a church no difference at all between a pagoda and between a church. Lucy Church is not insistent Lucy Church does not resemble Lucy Church does not desire to cultivate the acquaintance that has been begun between Elizabeth and Edith between Helen and Lilian between William and Sweet between Paul and John and between one at a time carefully. Lucy Church has made it not at all inordinate and has made it not at all that all the world in a colour between should be in books of porcelain and with very well interested desire to participate in it on that account. Please explain plainly that Lucy Church meant to come around.

Lucy Church and would Mrs. Hardy remember that her children had as their grandmother the more that it could be left to them to desire that if they were to arrange they would would prefer cats to kittens and

very little dogs to the one which when not at all troublesome they were annoyed and liked to be present when there was a pleasure in if it could be known that in sitting and in standing she was devoted and very much left it to them to be in no more than as they were careful it could be as well as might be in time to prepare to go because it is their delight to leave it as much as if they answered that they were there.

Lucy Church with what is known as very well and do please come to see if it is as much changed as it might have been if not only it was best of all as they could and would do to say so. Lucy Church can be thought to have been aware of their previously admiring white and black one at a time if it were made as suddenly as theirs in between. Lucy Church and with her unanimously as could and did did and could with it in in ineffable for instance would he be very pleased with saintly.

It was as much as if it as if it were to be in the meantime coming as by the time theirs were individually leaving leaving it in her possession in her possession when naturally surmounting coming to if on account of placing having an and surrounding a stairway which in undertaking and preserved to be served with when on and-in observation they might in their and in the midst with and with it all at all around might it be when if and beside not having not only down it is a virgin and a saw mill too. Two and two.

Lucy Church with wed and Wednesday and dead and Monday and said and Tuesday and had and Friday

142

and with and Sunday and might and Thursday. Saturday could be very well known as now they were occupied with the taking out and bringing earlier than later as it had to be there and here. You see to and can remember where they had it as much as if it was in use. In use in use. Lucy Church Lucy Church who knows how. Who knows how to bring in what is to be placed here so that it need not be brought in later. It is not brought in now because after all she was not ready to bring it in now.

Lucy Church and and beside that makes it even be to see even be to see seriously as seriously as even be to see seriously. Come and beside they need to have once in a while a disappointment in Simon Therese having grown thinner and whiter and so it is a disappointment to say so it is a disappointment to say so.

CHAPTER XVI

Did she know just what to say when she went away to-day which is a trick but we do not seem to be angry. Lucy Church which is why they have to believe that after all once in a while as it is very well to disposed of suddenly with it by the time as if when and because of it it is undertaken as not objectionable but merely with it as having been reduced in size.

Lucy Church made many admirable reflections upon whether it is better to have them rose and white blue and white brown and grey or all of it as it is planned and moreover as to meeting to meet. Do meet. Lucy Church to meet to meet do meet. Lucy Church do meet do meet with all the understanding that can be desired. Lucy Church do meet with all the understanding that can be desired. Lucy Church do meet with all all the understanding that that can be desired. Lucy Church do meet with all the understanding that can be desired.

Lucy Church do meet with all the understanding that can be desired.

Lucy in a minute and a minute Lucy Church Lucy in a minute in a minute and in a minute in a minute.

Lucy Church made a place on the part of the place where it is very well that it has happened that it is very partly this which and when there when there indefinitely could be as much as when they they in in and of a circumstance to adhere with and belying their intention to add an advantage to normally with and in as an elaboration of their really with it and now and then preferable. Coming to have two two parts of it. Coming coming. Very much as much as it is as if it were in a place of belittling it now.

Lucy Church could remain there did remain there was to remain there Lucy Church was to remain there is there and very much as much as much as can can be. Lucy Church very much as much as much as can be can be with it and with seldom with an in an appointed with it could and would. Lucy Church made it as much as if it could not be remembered.

Simon Therese could be called Emanuel. Simon Therese could be called Ferdinand Simon Therese could be called he could be called Simon Therese could be called so and could continue to look to see and could look to see and see and see that it is better to see that deer are deer and doves are doves and very small birds that feed on grain are very small birds that feed on grain and he was not interested at all not all at all.

John Mary might be a birthday he might.

John Mary might have had had and had had it had it had to also.

John Mary could be withstood by their elucidating

it to them it to them. John Mary with it and particularly particularly probably in their and in reference to the pleasure of at the side at the side is a hillside a hillside is by and by and not high as they say. It is like this a hill has been a hill and where it is where is it. Thank you so much.

Letting it remain that she likes it that it is very well understood that she that it is very well understood likes it.

A very little story of how very many have torn paper in order to make it do.

Lucy Church did not have a problem. She was one of three sisters who had not been born all of a sudden. She had been born the youngest and this was not considerably after any other. She had been once and once in a while very much as much as if and if and ever ever so much as much as much more. That is it.

Simon Therese is the youngest and there are more that can come to please a mother she prefers that they should be very well and very well I thank you and they and they are that is it is planned that they will go away as if as if they had all been gone not at all not at all not at all they are all as all and all all beside. To like to to like to to like to and to like to. Never to be asked have you heard me mention Lucy Church or Lucy Church or Lucy Lucy Church.

John Mary might very well very often might very often and as it is not William Mary not William Mary

and aloud. It is astonishing that unconciously John Mary and William Mary had an origin. It is surprising it surprised in telling as there had been unconciously that in in it in it in it now in it now that they they were if two came to cross which would go first. In and very likely. Come to be out and about.

CHAPTER XVII

William and Mary William Mary had been out and
out and out. Let him tell this William Mary tell him
William Mary let him William William Mary let him
tell him let him tell him this. William Mary was a
canon he was a canon and he was not invited and he
was to come and he came and he was to come and he
came and he had been and he had been William Mary
he had been. He had been and he was then a pleasure
to something something equivalent to right left and
everything William Mary and individually coffee and
individually wedding and individually acting and individually adding and individually left and left with
him left and left with him additionally left and with
him William Mary and his pleasure in this and this and
this and this and one and a million of individual addition. So then William Mary was not imbued with
it as was Lilian Stanhope who never knew that it was
better to leave it to them. It was better. To leave
it to them. Imbued with anything. It was better
to leave it to them. Could anybody think of her and

not know her name.   Could anybody think of her and
not know her name.   Could anybody think of her and
not know her name.   Could anybody think of her and
not know her name.   Two turtle doves can stand in
front of a standing photograph.

CHAPTER XVIII

Five leaves of five trees there are five trees and pampas grass. Five trees and five leaves and there is pampas grass. There is pampas grass and five leaves and five trees and they have a great many leaves on the trees. And so it is what is meant by leave it to me.

Simon Therese could be welcome at more than very much more than if she were as tall and as fair as when she might not like to have been not only not liking but waiting and being this to understand. To understand they undertake to overthrow their undertaking. This stand and to understand to undertake to undertake to overthrow to overthrow their undertaking.

Simon Therese had made them wait not wait for him not wait for them not wait for them he had made them wait not wait for them not wait for him not wait for him not wait for them. Simon Therese had not made them wait not made them wait not made them wait for them not made them wait for him had not made them wait for him had not made them wait for them. Simon Therese had not made them wait for him had not made them wait for them. Simon The-

rese had not made them wait for them had not made
them wait for them had not made them wait had not
made them wait for him had not made them wait had
not made them wait for them. Simon Therese had
not made them wait for them had not made them wait
had not made them wait for them. Simon Therese
had not made them wait for them.

If Annie Lyal was patient how did she like blankets.
If Alice Babette was sleeping how did she like adding.
If Adele Simonds was asking she asked how did she
like music.

How did she like asking how did she like adding
how did she like one half of one hundred how did she
like ivory needles how did she like white wool and sik
how did she like sitting how did she like liking it how
did she like coral how did she like adding this to that
and winning in opening opening it before before the
beginning of after it was as if it was in the morning and
so and so as much as it is very well not only to be but
to be to be placing it of them both there exactly it might
be remarked that it could be after the first then next
and next and back again and not in if at the more than
the second time briefly it was perhaps the third and
the third if not preferred chosen more than to cover
two which after it is to put it there there wherein it is
after it is partly and to cover at most it could be changed to at first and be more than one and some some of
it could be placed which when if not beside it is most
easily recognisable as left and right. Now and then
ten and ten ten two two and two although to you to

ten and ten ten and two two two to you to you. It should be and it was noted that it was after if it should be called four or five. And then could it be changed to one. It was. And across. Two across with across as across and not known known.

It is precarious that if it fits in a little cactus which is round and has fallen out and has been replaced with it as at once and given away that is a rosy one. One out of two.

Lucy Church can call curl curl and girl girl and pearl pearl and place place and at a distance at a distance and remarkably remarkably it can be possible that what is very large is very small if it is reduced what is very large is very small if it is reduced.

Lucy Church can not complain if he is told if he is told if he is told she can not complain if he is told if he is told if he is told if he is told about it and as he is told about it he knows that he is told about it and he knows that a whole regiment is in some countries four thousand men and in some countries is one thousand men and in some countries is twelve hundred men and in some countries is nine hundred men if he is told about it.

Lucy Church and adding, there is adding in there being in there being and leaving leaving it to them. There is adding in after in adding in after in adding in leaving in after in adding in leaving in leaving it to them. There is adding in after in adding in after in adding in leaving in after in adding in after in adding in leaving in leaving it to them. Lucy Church in after

in adding in adding in after in after in adding in after in adding in after in adding in adding in after in after in adding. Lucy Church in after in after in adding in after in adding in leaving in after in adding in leaving in after in adding leaving it to them.

Lucy Church in after in adding in leaving it in after in adding in leaving in after in adding in leaving it in leaving it in after in adding in leaving it to them.

Lucy Church in leaving it to them.

There was at one time no limit to it. There was no limit to it and there were just as often as they had more time they were adding whenever they could they were adding to it. At one time there was not any limit to it and at that time that they were not adding anything to it they were leaving it as they were leaving it for it and as they were leaving it for it they were adding they were adding that to it and they were adding that to it and they were leaving that for it and they were leaving it with it and they were adding it to it. At the time that there was no limit to it they were adding it to it they were adding it to it they were adding it to it at the time they were adding it to it they were adding this to it at the time they were adding this to it they were leaving this with it at the time that they were leaving this with it they were adding that to it they were adding it to it they were leaving this with it they were leaving it for it they were adding it to it. At the time that there was not any limit for it they were adding this to it they were leaving that for it they were leaving this to it they were adding that with it they

were adding to it with it with this to it. At the time
that there was no limit to it they were adding this to it.

If at most and best if most and best if most if most
and best how do they like to find it. They like to find.
How do they like to find it.

John Mary can know any Mary. John Mary can
know any Mary.

William Mary can know that they know that he
can know that they assist them at the same time.

John Mary can know any John or James Mary.
John Mary and James Mary. John Mary and James
Mary John Mary can know can know John Mary and
James Mary can know James Mary can know James
Mary and John Mary John Mary can know that there
is not very much snow that stays there as it is not high
enough to be cold enough and not north enough to be
cold enough and not near enough to the north to be cold
enough to make it disagreeable. John Mary can know
any Mary. James Mary not yet.

William Mary is not William Mary exactly. He
is not William Mary exactly. William Mary is William
and Mary exactly William Mary is William Mary
is William Mary is exactly is exactly not William and
Mary is William Mary. William Mary will not be
brought to be more than thoughtful. William Mary
will not be brought to be more than thoughtful.

John Mary establishes farms John Mary establishes
James. John Mary establishes John Mary establishes
farms. And so does his father. James Mary is the
brother of John Mary and perhaps he will be a help but

very likely it is not necessary that he does not come to stay away not at all agreeably and what is the difference if they like. James Mary if they alike. To ask ask ask it ask it ask to ask to ask to ask to ask it of them. It is more than a red berry to ask it of them. It is very much as if the flowers of a cactus would if they went on turn from rose to blue but do they do they do so or do they turn from blue to rose or do they remain blue and do they remain rose do they do so. This has nothing to do with any better way of adding stay away not any better way not any better way of adding not any better way of adding not any better way of adding stay away not any better way of adding not any better not any better way not any better way not any better way of stay away not adding.

It is a wish a wish of bone a wish bone. And so. To say. To say so.

CHAPTER XIX

In that case she will sit down quietly.

She will not thank for the wound wool as she has not noticed it it being the same colour as the chair and she having forgotten that she left it there. In that case she will be reminded of having heard them asking the time and her replying that it is a quarter of twelve and there being an answer to the effect that that is possible.

Lucy Church made many mountains made many mountains show in the distance she made many mountains show so that they could be seen at a distance this is useful and necessary if a river is supposed to overflow its banks it is useful and necessary if a river has tributaries which have overflowed their banks and have made it not possible to set fire to the growth that if not gathered for the bedding of animals would be more admired as having been set on fire in order that the folowing year it would grow higher. If the following year it would grow higher there is plenty of it more of it than they desire and the following year if the river has not inundated into it they will set it on fire again. Thank you very much.

Lucy Church in and on the side opposite to that where there has been this which has been admirably admired as a marsh. Lucy Church entirely and in a way to extend itself not only up and down and not over but not very much higher this is by the way. Lucy Church may be not only not in added estimation but please please let her know and let her have it known that it is as it was and very much as to fancy. She is to fancy that Frances Church can be the name by which she will be called. Frances Church is the sister of Lucy. This needs not remind one of her having to wait as she is changing from being remembered to having been remembered as to having been remembered differently being remembered as the same. Lucy Church seems to be seems to be seems to be seems to be seems to be seems to be seems to be not to be not to be seems not to be accustomed to having been influenced to be all there can be of there having been left to right with it irregularly and having been that is more than replaced by it. Thanks to this and a pleasure. It is very remarkable that going around and around up there and not going around and around here should be as if it could be that it was as actually left to it in replacing an ostrich egg with water and replacing and in replacing and in replying and in referring and in preference merely as when in integrally remonstrating when and by which it is very nearly replaced so also must it be by and by and as an occasion and occasionally within and delight and relight it is not inconvenient to disturb Fontainebleau.

Lucy Church was never there naturally naturally she was never there. And so they with with in in and beside in it and for instance in obliging and obligation having secured with it in and around and moreover it is a pleasure plainly a pleasure and a triumph. My daughter will never say it again my daughter will never be there again my daughter will never sing again and very likely and very likely it was in answer.

Lucy Church had been to church. She had been to church now that it was possible. She had been to church Lucy Church had been to church now that it was possible. Frances Church had been to church had been to church now that it was possible. Lucy Church now that it was possible had been to church. Lucy Church now had been to church now that it was possible. Who has been in who has been in in church now that it was possible. Lucy and Frances Church have been in church have been in church have been in church now that it is possible.

CHAPTER XX

Not to-day.

Simon Therese not to-day.

Simon Therese not to-day Simon Therese any way.

Simon Therese has made more money than he could if he had invented things that made black and white be as much as if it had been best to have it as their share. He did like very much more than he had had as it was very nearly as much a pleasure as it had been to him for them and believing believing that it was not at that time that there is a difference between an Arab village and a garage is it if it is built to be nearly as near to the center of this city which is theirs to sit up to lie down and to walk around gradually with it and very much to like and alike and as to like and very likely and adaptably and much of it much of it much of it very much of it very much of it and to be sure to be to be sure to be sufficiently as well as sufficiently as well as as well as sufficiently. As well as sufficiently.

Simon Therese was not Simon Therese he was not Simon Therese because his face had gotten thinner

and because he was not Simon Therese she found it oftener than ever she found it oftener than ever better to ask him how does your mother like it that it is partly more theirs than before and how many are there of them there then and so it was much more than they had ever liked it before very much more. He was not lingering he never had made very many made as many made as very many made he did not attribute it to this and there not having been asked at that time this and this question and this and this answer and being perfectly very much pleased that if they had been left to them left to them or left to them or left to them. How many are there left of them there are all of them left of them and there are all of them left of them and there are all of them left of them. There are all of them left of them there are left all of them are left of them. Simon Therese might be one of one two there might be one of one two might be one of one might be one of one one one one two three one might be one might be one of one. Simon Therese and he might be might be and he might be and he might be might be he might be he might he might be he might be he might be he might be one of one he being one of one he was very much in and as if it was which one which one did one and one is one one one one one and one. Simon Therese one Simon Therese one Simon one Simon Therese one.

Simon Therese it is not to be not to be not to be not to be Simon Therese made no mountains out of it having been that large and as many coming coming to be

in liquidate liquidate liquidate paint paint went went went to before before that this there they beside beside with went went and in in and as if it is could have to be excellent excellent with which it is very useful to be taken care of.

Simon Therese cried.

It is very much too much to be very much too much to be very much as if it is a pleasure to be said to be in the after it has been and coming theirs as the left to it in and and become become become to be sure coming with it in it in it to be certain can and will will it in a afternoon afternoon readily readily in ambush it is allowed in ambush ambush and a cactus which has been bought has been bought and if alive has been given away as it is readily fading and if it is readily fading a little round one and a little round one and a little and a little round one. It is more than with it with it in and in and in and in a left to it very little more than which it can be could could be liking a description of nature which has a river and and better and a little and very well I thank you and they and honey honey and accacia and tobacco and dahlia and a little and with it with it if it turned its back very well upon all who came feeding very well upon all who came feeding very well.

Simon Therese is a very well impressed addition to their sing and a song and never has been heard never never very well never.

Simon Therese has decided to go and see Spain Italy Germany and Egypt and he had told Mary so he

has told Mary so and Mary has not been told so he has told Mary so and everybody was there and so it was not only that he would go but not go this year.

Alike it is more alike than it was. It is more alike than it was. It is more alike than it was.

It made two noises one of the first dropping of something and the second of the dropping of something. It made two noises. It made a noise the dropping of something. There were two noises. In an amount of which it is left to this with it more and can be and is as if in and beside inclined to be in in profussion preference to in bereft of theirs in a chance to chance to a chance to a chance and left to follow please and to please and to please to please with it cordially left to right join it there there in place place and can can if in in it. Regrettably.

Simon Therese can use having been seated and left. He left. Slowly. Slowly and adding. Adding and by and by. By and by with him. He was asking if sundries could be added to by not a deception for him. Nothing is a deception for him. Nothing is a deception for him.

Foreign for him. He could be left to be planned as twenty once in a while once in a while once in a while. Once Once in a while.

Simon was never more than he could be if he had at no time to be said to be said to be said to be away. Said to be away.

Simon Therese made many many made many many. Simon Therese made Simon Therese came when he was

162

invited and he said. I will come. He came when he was invited. He said I will come. He came when he was invited. He said he said I will come. What has she to do with it she is not a member of the family. He came and Simon Therese he came and Simon Therese he came he came when he was invited. He said he would come. He came when he was invited.

Beginning with Simon Therese and ending with he came when he was invited.

CHAPTER XXI

There is a better than best best and most and she did. So they say.

Lucy Church came to know Helen. That is Helen drank pansies.

Lucy Church perhaps later when she too had been interrupted in having commenced to call would also as she was not at all would also would also as she would not as she not at all as she would if it were as it is heard she came she called and she was then not by pleasure and it amused her. It was useful too. Because if they came there there was when if they had but they did and it was not the habit to give it to them it was not the habit to give it to them even if they wished to. Very much more not likely very much more not likely.

Lucy Church could be advantageously left to be so that it is very delightful that it is pleasant.

If he were very well not well and he changed from one place to the other could it be by any accident that having come to be there and by that an opportunity to be older older and his hair softer and older and staying longer and older and not remaining better

would he be very welcome not to remember that after all Egypt is Egypt and Algeria Algeria and Wyoming Wyoming and Belley Belley. And so to know that Belley is Belley and as far away as if they were very naturally industrious and a pleasure.

There is no use in asking him to have a memory for who had been heard to say how do you like it now that you are so much better and having it happen exactly as you had expected. There are many parts of places.

It is not more left to them to say again that it is called so much called so that very happily there being saints it is not necessary to repeat names. Letting alone names. Some letting alone names put it away some letting alone names put it away from one to three some letting alone names put it away from not liking a difference between a quarter and a third and there are some who like it very much. Lucy Church could be in and in and in and in and reminded and in and reminded and inundated.

If anybody had two and one of the two one of the two that is there had been an a hiatus a hiatus makes meadows scarce makes trees be chestnut trees instead of poplars and plane trees and make pansies wild and late in drying and honey is best when it is only once not once or twice. All of which is of no interest.

To interest.

What very slowly what very slowly what did you say.

It is very well that it is of no interest. To some

capital is of no interest to some interest is of no interest.

Very slowly it is of no interest.

Very slowly what did you say.

Very slowly it is of no interest.

Very slowly it is of no interest.

Very slowly what did you say.

It is by no means useful to have been called just the same.

If they come and if they go nobody knows that it is so.

Very likely.

If they come if she has come that means that she has gone out and come back again.

If she has gone out and come back again she has brought back something unless she was unable or unwilling to be after all actively engaged in that occupation. It is not at all very likely.

It might be partly that she would be very much as much as much as if she did.

She did what she liked.

They made all of it as well as they ever had and do they worry about it. Not at all. It is not much of an undertaking. Do they worry about it. Not at all.

Let every one think about a Ford car. In the life time of a man they have changed their mind. Very well I thank you.

In the life time of a man they have changed their mind. Who might they be. In a life time of a man they have changed their mind who might they be.

So many so many so many so and so.

Lucy Church could be Lucy Pagoda and not change her mind. It is very likely that Lucy Church in a way Lucy Church in a way Lucy Church in a way did not cannot cannot change her mind. Lucy Church.

Lucy Church made a way between and on the side of a river of a river of a river. Lucy Church made the way made the way made made the way on the side at the side of a river of a river that had high banks. High banks can be compatible with canals. High banks can be compatible with Lucy Church surmounted by a pagoda. Lucy Church can be compatible with banks that are sufficiently high to have beyond the road hills that are not only higher but have fairly large trees growing on them. If they are higher they are not there.

Lucy Church is just beyond where the river turns. Lucy Church is just beyond where the river makes a bend. Lucy Church is just beyond where the river having made a bend there is a bridge and not at all an other bridge. This one connects one side of the river with the other.

Lucy Church could be and can be not be and need be need be and they are to be she is to be if there are to be any births any marriages and any marriages and any births there is the family and there is a family if there are any marriages and any births. Very well I thank you.

Lucy Church in summer and Lucy Church in winter. Lucy Church made it be very well know that what is prepared is prepared beforehand and what is

given is given beforehand and what is left is left beforehand and unexpectedly.

If in buying a fort they speak of it will they run into the gate. The fort is for sale. Thank you very much.

This is directly not of interest to Lucy Church although there is a possibility that indirectly it may be of importance to her indirectly.

Afterwards neither she nor John Mary occasionally heard about it. She was beside that more than having an intention. And he he would if it were not for that be there.

John Mary makes it be very much as much as if he had been not only but and with with it as soon. It might be left to be very much with it with it and made to be made to be with it with it as if it were of no extra relief to have it heard. If a father and a mother are dead is there an orphan if there is in each case one child. And if they should later have two sons and each one of them one after the other is there is there there is an opportunity to be gradually as if it is a decided agreement to remain that is to be succeeded by one another.

Let it leave let it be as leave let it be let it be as leave it leave eaten leave in leave in eaten. In in in as much as much as they they they to be sure with could and belief that if four they were mistaken it had been that the sister was simple minded and played with her father. It takes two a father and a mother to have four sons and one daughter and the daughter

very pretty and very likely to be exactly what she expected.

They might be all day about it.

Left to each teach preach left to each. It is left to each to have to be mistaken in the thought which is the result of conversation ⸱that perhaps they would have to earn it. They liked to be all told.

Pleasures in having it changed from there not needing to their needing to to their not needing to. Nevertheless they say that they cannot go away no not even to be told so. They are not told so because having been told they say they have been told so and they had suspected it. They having suspected they when the opportunity came they when the opportunity came they did what was forced upon them and they might regret it. If they did it would be difficult and if they did not it would be difficult.

Every little while once in a while, if there are three and one is older the second one will have to be older and it will take longer that is there are as many years to wait as late.

It is as much as they can be believed to find interchangeable one two three all out but she. Lucy Church went away but not as often as she had been very much to be sure. Very very much to be sure. Are you sure.

CHAPTER XXII

One two three one two three one two three four and no more. They are an asset.

Why has no one written the biography of the man who thought of and made the soap that floats. It would be interesting.

In a minute.

It would be that they were that it is that they can be more interesting not more interesting but more different very much as much as much different as it is not possible to think of it that is that he did, he did think of it as much as if it had been that both his mother and his father died in an accident. His father and his mother died in an accident as much as it is as much as it is as much and as different as different as it is but is it as it is as it is told if it is asked did it happen not is it as much as if they were to be retarded could it be the most worth while of them all. All in all.

Sweet peas whose seeds have been given to him have been very well grown and they are when even there are as few delicately rose without any blue more than

suggestible very much more curly than they were before this kind. They are so kind that they like this kind and they like this kind as they are so kind.

William Mary and partly to care partly to care for Harry Mary and Henry William Mary he said he might be named after him. It is very much as best and most that they were with with and all all and better better and now now and around with and look there is a more admired way of making fountains than just around and about than just books in porcelain than just does it happen to be theirs especially than just what they were to do in order to make glass blue than just as much as if and by nearly very nearly comparing having it left to them in the meantime in the meantime just in time.

Do you think it at all likely that he will come without letting her know.

Colour to be the colour to be chosen is if he asked what colour is it.

The colour to be if the colour to be chosen is the colour of which he asked what colour is it.

It is very well and possibly very very well to have her say not at all as if it is to be asked will he be there and oversee the two or three actually three of which two of them are each four and one of them two and around and around there are some to be renewed some to be excused some to be hopefully exactly as they were. Everybody hopes so because it will be very much less of an annoyance if it is so.

Lucy Church made a frank refusal of why there is in a way an error in her partly being there entirely.

She made a frank refusal and a denial and because of the denial it is true partly true that because and the cause can justify that feeling. The feeling makes it play that it is as much as they can say. If it can be seen from there is it there. Exactly. If it is seen from there is it there. Exactly. If it is seen from there is it there. Exactly. If it is seen from there and it is there it is here if it is seen from there. It is seen from there. Exactly. If it is seen from there it is here and it is here it is seen here it is seen here it is seen to be here it is seen from there and so a river is so and so. Exactly. A river is so and so. Exactly. Partly. Exactly. Well. Exactly. Partly well well partly exactly. It is partly well partly partly well partly well exactly it is partly partly exactly. It is there here and here and there exactly. Very satisfactory exactly.

A river is in place of here and there exactly.

Here and there exactly in place of Lucy Church to be sure to be navigable to be sure to be sure to be sure to be Lucy Church to be sure that a very little. A very large. A very large exactly.

Come to be come to be.

Right and left. Left and right. Come to be.

To put into a book what is to be read in a book, bits of information and tender feeling.

How do you like your two percent bits of information and tender feeling. She said that she was to be

satisfied with that and she was and later she was re-
warded she was able to be very much interested by
what they had done with them and as much as much
as it is very much very much which is very much which
is it that it is to be preferably as they indicate theirs
individually and as pleasure as if it is more than it is
in case of in relation and because of it with it as it is
around.

He was very well pleased that she was there in
plenty of time to have it as a decided refual of their
willing to be gone alone and how do you like it how do
you like how do you like it.

To be very much influenced by intending to fairly
well led to be more than it is as if they wished to be
one at a time in consequence in consequence of it.

Did they say that they knew better.   They did.

Albert Bigelow some of the time in mine.

Could iron.

Very well.

By the window.

Albert Bigelow could iron very well by the window.

And the light might in as well and if there were more
and more which is a finer than ever that they had.

Albert Bigelow and Emil Henry and William Mary
never met. This was natural is natural as Albert
Bigelow and William Mary met. This is natural as
Emil Henry never has needed to see that if he could
not need that a woman must have to go where he would
not care to have to spend his time as he was very well
prepared and was it as seen. He had relatives in

Caesarieux. Where they have Madeleine and Madeleines and bread and teaching that is one and one. One is not yet to be in three years after and the other very nearly as much as never observing that the marshes having every winter a fire need observation as they often have in the fall an inundation and sometimes in the summer which is grievous as it destroys the potatoes which however are not planted there only nearly there but it is inconvenient for cows to be deprived of bed, not absolutely impossible but disagreeable and so to be so to be so to be as much as if there is not to be known as part of the time in which meant to arrange.

It is more than they meant as they went.

Please pay well please pay as well please pay as well as what is it.

Letting him be painting on glass and not thinking of painting on glass.

Letting him be thinking of not being willing to be paying to have him be beginning to be painting to be asking to be painting on glass. Painting on glass alas.

Painting on glass makes it be jewelry. So he is to be advised to be having to be known to be very well to be very well I thank you.

John Mary joined wheat to more wheat and he is very well pleased with the result. So is all France.

Here and there so is all France.

Here and there so is all France.

John Mary has joined everything to it and he is slowly slowly coming to be known as staying at home slowly to be known as staying at home and milk.

Milk of human kindness.

Thank you and esteem he will esteem it a favour if he is visited and what he has done is approved he will also esteem it a favour if he has not done so. He will also be favourably alarmed by their return of once every once in a while as much as if as usual having been fearful of it turning as it might but rarely does it makes no difference as they do not mind having had it as habitual and it in no way deterring from its strength.

As round and about.

Why do they never give away winter clothes but only summer clothes.

They have more houses than villas and more places than meadows. Meadows gradually are green and so are poplars as you say.

An interval between Simon Therese and William Therese and Arthur Therese and Hilda Therese and John Therese. A space between William Mary and Albert Bigelow and a son who can be part of the time which was after it was partly there and theirs in their pleasure to have to be not as much not by the time not to be more than easily frightened.

CHAPTER XXIII

Lucy Church can be added to a little by then.

They said it was to be expected.

If in between it is as much as they had and could did and left left to it as with in it is to be settled settlement.

It made it be theirs too.

Two and as much.

With and believe.

It is Mrs. Wiedner who said did you know that it was I.

CHAPTER XXIV

If men have not changed women and children have.
If men have not changed women and children have.
If men have not changed women and children have.

CHAPTER XXV

If men have not changed women and children have.
Men have not changed women and children have.
Men have not changed women and children have
changed.

Simon Therese could and would would would and
could could did and would would would and could
could did and could would. He would if he were not
to be taught to be letting it down and being on it as it
is it is it that it is that it is attached.

And so he and it it did not did not need to have to
have the paint cleaned off cleaned off the panels of
glass.

Panels of glass not alas.

He meant to be crowned crowned with Simone.
Simone and is it very well known that it can be as
much as fourteen. Fourteen as much as fourteen.
Fourteen as much as fourteen within in searching. In
exchange for there.

There is a part of it in colour a part of it in colour
a part of it in colour. There is a part of it in colour.

Simon Therese in case in case of all day.

Simon Therese could be very well well told well told welcome well told well told well told and not at all Louis' brother. Louis' brother was another and not Simon Therese at all whether whether in and for and now now and then and with and can candid with them.

He might be told that nobody knew.

Shrewdly.

He might be told that nobody knew shrewdly.

But she said did you do it have you done it and very much as when there is a discovery it is very well known that it is not to be found then. Then and then. Who has been known as yesterday neither here nor there.

Older the do not change but because there is an answer they can give an answer. And older they can give an answer they can give an answer there is an answer.

Older there is an in and and and in there is and in an answer.

Thank you very much for being wealthy and famous.

CHAPTER XXVI

They were twice women.

Any twice is once or twice and who can say that in every day or two there is an acquaintance. And acquaintance which might be left to out loud. They can be occasionally very much without it.

Let no one know how they told it so that it was unexpected. Unexpected.

Let no one have it as partly that.

Let no one cloud a very hazy day as is repeatedly what is a great regret that now that they are here they are very pleased.

Plainly in case of having heard heard it with and without it being more than very much as much as completely in theirs and circular. A circular play is a play in circles and they are there he and higher she and beside. And so with it as at once.

There are very many eatables in it as it is made to hold muscat grapes. There are very many eatables as it as it is gunpowder tea. It is that there are very many eatables as it is that there are valley birds. It is that there are very many eatables as it is that there

are very many if they ask in autumn they ask in autumn if they ask in winter they ask in winter if they ask in between there comes to be partly a risk. Of course there comes partly a risk. Of course of course there comes there comes partly of course of course there comes partly there comes partly a risk. Of course of course of course there of course there comes partly a risk. She was principally a seen principally at a distance at a time very many say and said so. Who was told to be very much as if they had said not at all.

Not at all makes it be whether or whether it is what they wanted.

Want and wanted it is always very well known that the north of a country is more north than the south of country that is more north. And this is as is older.

Lillie do you understand.

Lilian St Peter and might say repeatedly repeatedly.

It could be forth and forth.

CHAPTER XXVII

How many no doubt are there of it.

How many no doubt.

He would not have it and he said so he would not have it and he knew that he knew it.

This is because it is never to be best and most now is it. Lilly and Lilian and Lily Agnes. They came within an ace of sailing. An ace is to say so.

Lucy Church having forgotten a river knows that a river is very much longer than wider and very much quicker than ever. Not at all.

It is very much what and what to say.

She said that it was why they had been left to it.

CHAPTER XXVIII

Something a thousand and twenty and my asking what is it.

Anybody can be older if their eyes are smaller. Anybody can be older if their eyes are smaller. Lucy Church might be three and three.

Anybody can be older if their eyes are smaller.

Three and three makes forty-three.

Forty three makes two and two two and three. Thirty-three and forty forty three makes their eyes smaller if they are older. If they are older are their eyes smaller or are their faces bigger. Three and three if their eyes are smaller or their faces are larger or if they are older. This can be said of very beautiful men and very beautiful women.

Lucy Church saw her mother lead them as is natural if to walk in front of them and they walk quicker and if another one is to walk quicker and they are to then walk quicker will Lucy Church's mother add them and ask them if they mind about it and if so and if so they would be so and it had not been as is very often not the case as in any case unless they are going the other

way they are either standing still or not at all altogether. It is in a way in a way so and so necessarily as is the habit of it in respect to their being more than if when and carry then.

It is that makes mountains it is that that it is this that it is this that makes mountains out of it is this out of it is it is this.

Lucy Church if she were to be her acquaintance Helen Helen in founding something something in founding finding in finding founding founding that that that it was to look through look through through across. How many have been given.

It is very likely.

They may.

Lucy Church made it Lucy Lucy Church.

Lucy Church who made it.

Made it.

Lucy Church at with made see more see more two more two more or, or if it were as in that better seen when in in in between coming to be two three.

Lucy Church could never find Helen, Mary, Helen. Lucy Church could never find Helen Mary.

Helen Mary how many how many Helen Marys are there to be had as many as every time every every time time of day Helen Mary made it in pieces made it in made it in in preparation in then then to to to be shown. It was why they had it.

Helen Mary makes it be that if partly because because of blows blow which shine as weather whether in abundance. It was to be seen to farther. Helen

Mary can be conducted to it now now and then. It is as much as could could it be helped. It could and would.

Helen Mary can Helen Mary can can be as much as if with it as to be left to them inimitably.

Helen Mary would not be found there.

She followed would not be found there.

Helen Mary she followed would not be found there. Helen Mary she followed would not be found there.

An and to be.

William Mary could be a wonderfully seen event of them of them could be a could be a wonderfully could be be seen event of them. As to two.

William Mary they might buy a house. One that had been built. And had been newly roofed as very many houses are if they have not been in order to prevent having had had it. It is very well known as history just as well known. William Mary very addedly carefully carefully to be to be it is as well to have it like it. Like it like that. William Mary and with and withstand he did not endow withstanding admittedly admittedly with them. With them. In a minute. William Mary in branches.

Does it make any difference if a silhouette changes every ten years. Lucy Church made it not obligatory as they say so.

Helen Mary Helen Mary Helen Mary had had been been tall. Thank you very much.

CHAPTER XXIX

There are two ways two a day. Two days.
Come again.

CHAPTER XXX

Surely yes.

Yes surely.

How many times can they be there.

Once.

How many times can they be there with them.

Once.

How many times can they be there with them and not be there again.

Once.

Thank you very much.

Information.

It is the very best that they can.

William Mary would have become William Mary.

Yes he would.

John Mary would be John Mary.

Lucy Church can be Lucy Church.

Lilian can bring Lily.

And Helen can be this Helen and that Helen.

This Helen and that Helen.

Once in a while they are partly very confidently

and the unexpected arrival of having heard it when it came.

Twice as long.

Not to be exactly very well and very well and very well how do you like it.

It is partly conjecture it is partly conjecture.

He succeeded in having Simon Therese having now to be after when and where they were made to be carried they inclined to be wishing that it was as surrounded as it had been and Simon Therese does know the difference in oceans.

CHAPTER XXXI

In fact in fact in the life in fact in the life and after all in fact after all after all which is it after all which is it.

It is as if they could be known.

To be thrown.

It is as if they could be known to be thrown away in Spanish and if in Spanish then how many years is it.

If it is when they were flattered how flattered were they.

At last at first and best and most how did they know that it was chilly and unpleasant if they were asked to have it be left to them and it is and it is when he came and asking was not very often in a while in a while as often.   It is very easy to minister to William Mary.

He wanted to examine it and he was waiting for it and he was after a very little awhile just as anxious about it and he was not at all delighted with there not being many more than they had in leaving it.

Very close to the more than they had to have it be

what after a while would be because it would be scrutinised. Very nicely.

To repeat the action how many arrangements are placed in the same afternoon advantageously as they are as very likely as not to be very often inadvertently complimentary but just at once Simon Therese just at once with them fortunately quite a lot of it as there is more than every reason for that mistake and not to be made with it and because of it when they came in.

He opened the door and walked in that is in the morning and in the evening and in the afternoon exactly.

He could easily forget to care if Lily and Lily and let it alone as they were to be very much as much as much as it is where they were still crossing it out as not being very well placed there in spite of it.

Lucy Church at once recognised the sound she heard which in incidentally relieving it could be that now there had never been at this time more than previously gathered as for instance it must be have it to be there.

Would she too be too busy to know that it is as much as if they having it partly in that as a difficulty once again never having seen it as closely nevertheless if in front of it there was there and not nearer how many many open squares and places are there in it. This makes what is it fortunately in reappearing.

Many many have to have to have it. And allowed.

There is one thing that is perfectly satisfactory. They do not like to know why they like another another what another adding of in in it.

Thank you very much.

CHAPTER XXXII

It is an ostrich egg in wood and a favourable straw and a favourable straw and a favourable straw favourable as to favourable as to it. Favourable as to it. As favourable as to it.

Lucy Church may be may be she will not notice it more than she would have if she would have been here would have been would have been would have been away from when when is it that that there is more of it in the meantime when they have been as much and as often as hearing hearing and heard hearing. Thank you thank you very much.

They were pleased.

CHAPTER XXXIII

Do wish her here.

Every little while Albert Bigelow was not only very attentive but he looked lost.

Every little while Lilian St. Peter Stanhope was methodical.

Every little while once in a while they might admire them one at a time.

Every little while it was an indication of whether it was not only very much better for them to believe in Helen Mary and what is it. It is an interruption. She had come to be more than careful.

After that out loud. Allowed. Potatoes can be pulled or dug out of the ground and transported, they can be transported to where they will be used a month at a time. Very well cake. Durable. Lucy Church and another mother who had as a daughter Therese and her sister who could be very welcome if at first very much first and last and all the time as is very well known to be meant to be carefully undertaken. It is all of that.

Lucy Church can be authentically managing to finish it just as well as ever just as well as ever.

Coming to come back.

If it surprises him that there are only sixty generations between him and Jesus Christ why does it surprise him.

It has surprised him that there are only four generations between him and Wellington not four only three it has not surprised him but once in a while before it did not surprise her because she calculated it all out and she was surprised.

All this will and willingly willingly and very well very well and as well and to be on the scent of how many how many are there in it and religiously there was no objection no objection to a renewal of it in replacing attachments with there having not been any of at it any time and there was if in including it smaller there is inevitably a very little handle of leather leather whether whether it is reproached by a very thin shaving of it in having it more than more than little holes. On the whole. Very much.

There is no need of wondering how old is Lucy Church nor William Mary nor if you like it Simon Therese nor if nor if nor if you like Sarah Frederic nor if you like it Sarah Frederic nor if you like nor if you like it with it because because continually because continually either either or or made to be formerly in use in use to use chocolate chocolate with sugar prepared for more there is more there is there when when is it to be made to be made usefully usefully to be released as

an object to which there can be no objection since
since it is when there can be after there has been all
of it in influence and influenced by them to be left to
them advantageously with it and bound bound to be
alike and liking, did they feel it to be partly to fall to
fall have fallen it fell this always can be green and
leaves and after a little while poplar. Poplars leave
tracks.

How many have heard of it. As many as can come
to be known as Spaniards from South America one at a
time and two were there and these make it delightful
of course make it delightful.

Simon Therese in case in case that he was very
much occupied and attracted by lectures on Africa.

Simon Therese because he was very well pleased
that if his mother was satisfied with the situation of
his younger and youngest brother.

In spots it is very identical in spots and very much
with it when it when it was and when it went there.

Lucy Church made witnesses witness an inundation
of the river Rhone. There has been nothing mentioned
about it because usually it happens and very often they
know that tributaries as is usual as is usual as is peaceful as is peaceful as is happily as is happily they are
how many are there now present after there has been
every effort made to gather them together.

CHAPTER XXXIV

Lucy Church is perhaps to be as well as ever in the estimation of those who remembered that fifteen years before she was slimmer and happily vigurously arousing their pleasure in being neither in front nor in the middle of those walking from there to there. Those walking from there to there.

John join join lead lead it to the back to them. Who when. When is it. What is it. Who is it.

Lucy Church might be as very well distanced by Lucy Church might be as very well distanced as by as by as by as well Lucy Church might as well be as well as well distanced as well Lucy Church might be as well as well distanced Lucy Church might be as well distanced.

CHAPTER XXXV

It is as roses that cows commit suicide.

It is as lilies that it is as lilies and lilies and as lilies that cows that cows commit commit suicide.

It is as roses it is as rose roses that cows that cows commit commit suicide.

It is as roses that cows commit commit suicide.

Simon Therese could know could come could come could come could refuse could please could please could fan could fan could could see could leave could with it all could at all be here.

Lucy Church could not be here she never had been here. She never could be here. She never would be here. Lucy Church could never be here. Lucy Church here here Lucy Church there Lucy Church Lucy Church and gaining she is gaining this from that and after it after it to them. Can Lucy Church distinguish a river. All the same.

William Mary and a cloud a cloud has a view a view and if he called John he not knowing his name would not call John Mary John Mary.

William Mary met and ate.

There are a great many relations between six at once and three at once. How do you do. Very well I thank you. And how were you prepared. Very well prepared. And when is it to be when is it to happen again. Not at this time. No not at this time.

They are usually undisturbed.

CHAPTER XXXVI

After this the end of the season bouquet little daisies little bluettes and a little hypatica and if yellow was allowed any number of very little yellow flowers very little yellow flowers, daisies very little bluettes a very small anemone and very little yellow flowers very many very little yellow flowers and very little clover and a few yellow asters if yellow is allowed which it is not.

Very little daisies and very little bluettes and an artificial bird and a very white anemone which is allowed and then after it is very well placed by an unexpected invitation to carry a basket by an unexpected invitation to carry a basket back and forth back and forth and a river there is this difference between a river here and a river there. There is this difference between a river here and a river there. Listen. There is this difference between a river here and a river there.

John Mary might be thin and have been when he came and passed by and when he passed by and he came. John Mary might have been thin then and might be called thin in Europe when he came to be then and then then and then thin and then and collected and

collecting. It is very much better to have been passing when he went that way. Did he. Very well
I thank you.

John Mary elaborately and with and withal and
John Mary with this with this is with this married
married with this and very much obliged and comes
to go and comes to go and comes to go and to say so.
Never having met another John Mary because his
brother James Mary is younger than his brother John
Mary.

There are many ways to pay a day, pay a day and
pay away and pay away and pay a day. How much
did Albert Bigelow say it cost. Fifty nine francs.
How much did Albert Bigelow say that it cost. Fifty
nine francs and having received one hundred francs he
gave back forty-one francs. How many francs did
Albert Bigelow say that it cost. Albert Bigelow did
not say anything he had one hundred francs given to
him and he gave forty one francs back every evening
after he had paid for everything.

John Mary was never to have anything matter.
John Mary was never to have anything matter and
whether and whether there was better better than ever.
Better than ever. John Mary was never to have anything matter. John Mary was never to have anything
matter. As everything that is now that his father
was weaker and he had made everything better now
that his mother was weaker and they had made
everything better now that John Mary was never
to have anything matter it was frequently that

he was married to Mary. It was frequently that
he was married to Mary. It was frequently that he
was married to Mary. John Mary was married to
Mary, Mary Mary and they had three children all three
girls, Helen Mary the oldest and she was just as old
as when after some time she was married and Elsie
Mary who was not the oldest and if it was said that
she was like Felicite who would take care of her brother
if she had a brother who would be apt to be very much
after he had gone away not to stay but to do what
would be delayed practically and afterwards the youngest would be known so Frances Mary would be known
so and that year three would be born there and they
would be very much what it was at a place known as
well as if they were known to be as much older. Frances Mary would be known to be as much older and she
would be known to be known to be as much so much
younger and therefor therefor there is no necessity of
there having it to do thanks thanks to this thanks to
this too thanks to this thanks to this to this too thanks
to it.

Might it be that they were not asking them to leave
it alone.

CHAPTER XXXVII

Paper and paper pay her.
Pay her pay her for the paper.
Pay her for the paper.
By her pay her pay her pay her for the paper.
Lucy Church was astonished to know that they loved her so was astonished to know that to pay her to pay her to pay her so to pay her for the paper to pay her they loved to pay her. They did love to pay her they loved to pay her for the paper. They loved to pay Lucy Church for the paper. They loved to pay her. They loved to pay her for the paper.

CHAPTER XXXVIII

This is why they loved to pay her for the paper. This is why they loved to pay her for the paper. They loved to pay her for the paper. This is why they loved to pay her for the paper.

CHAPTER XXXIX

It is once in a while that they like it best. Most and best did she say. It is once in a while that they like it best best best most and best did she most and best once in a while. It is once in a while that they like it best.

Lucy Church is a modest girl and when she is an old woman she having been an old woman and a modest girl will like it best. Of course she will like it best. She will like it best just as she is and as she will like best just as she is she will of course she will she will like it best. She will like it best.

If she is a modest girl she will like it and she is a modest girl and she will like it. When she is and she is she is an old woman she is an old woman and she likes it she likes it she likes it she likes it best she likes it best she likes it of course she likes it, she likes it. In between how many have been in between in between when there has been much of it much of it after it has been with it and because because to like it because because of course because of course because of course because because she does like it. She does like it. Lucy Church does like it.

CHAPTER XL

There is scarecely more than there is. There is there is scarcely more than there is.

There is more scarcely more than there is of it with it without there having been scarcely more than there is of it.

Lucy Church may laugh about it. She may laugh about it because it is the very best material there is and plenty of it and sometimes the last of it. She may laugh about it because if there is as much of it as there has to be to have it last as long as it does it is of very much greater use to her than to them than to them than to her. She is in many ways their equal.

She is in many ways their equal and equal and equal and equably and in a great many ways their equal their equal.

In many ways their equal she is in many ways their equal.

When Lucy Church was and is in many ways their equal. Lucy Church when Lucy Church when Lucy Church when Lucy Church in many ways is their equal

when Lucy Church is when Lucy Church is in many ways their equal.

The nineteenth century was English the eighteenth century was french the seventeenth century was dutch the sixteenth century was Spanish the fifteenth century was Italian and so forth. Lucy Church and so forth. Neglected and so forth. Very much and so forth. In a minute and so forth. A bouquet and so forth. Two at a time and so forth. Lucy Church and so forth. Lucy Church administering a river and so forth. A river and so forth. Once in a while and so forth. Very well I thank you and so forth.

Lucy Church is two years older and she was two years older and so forth.

Lucy Church made it just as much as when if in intermediate they had made a mistake about Chambery and he had made a mistake about Chambery and she had not made a mistake about Chambery. She had not made a mistake about Chambery she knew the exact distance that Chambery was from there and that Bourg was from there. Bourg was the place which being very well and very detailed in their expectation could include their education could include their education. Could it include their education. Could include their education.

Chambery could not include their education. And why. Because it is very well known that to be further known that to be further known there and there.

This is within which whose this is within which.

Lucy Church made a went away asked again as with

it with it in and on and on account of it. Mention another one mention Grenoble. I will mention another one I will mention Grenoble. Mention another one mention Grenoble I will mention another one I will mention Grenoble.

Mention another one. They made it have it have it here have it as if with within.

Lucy Church has been Lucy Pagoda has been Lucy Pagoda has been Lucy Church has been neither Lucy Church has been nor Lucy Pagoda has been neither Lucy Pagoda has been nor Lucy Church has been neither Lucy Church has been nor Lucy Pagoda has been neither Lucy Pagoda has been neither Lucy Church has been seen neither Lucy Church has been seen neither Lucy Pagoda has been seen.

Lucy Pagoda found it out found out Lucy Church found out found it found it out found it out found it found out that neither Lucy Church has been seen that neither Lucy Pagoda has been seen in winter. Neither Lucy Church nor Lucy Pagoda have been seen in winter.

Lucy Church may be very well accustomed to their being there Lucy Church may be very well accustomed may be very well accustomed here and there to their being there.

Lucy Church when this happens.

Lucy Church liking it.

Lucy Church liking it. Lucy Church Lucy Church liking it.

Lucy Church liking Lucy Church liking it.

This is every difference between hearing and seeing

and seeing and hearing both at once and if it is that going and going makes it undeniable undeniable is not allowed not only allowed not only not not only allowed.

Lucy Church in in delight. How many are there to be sent. Lucy Church in in delight. Lucy Church in in delight. How many are there to be sent. Lucy Church in in in delight in delight how many are there how many are there to be sent. Lucy Church in in delight.

Surely you are very stupid not to be secure about it surely you are very stupid not to be secure about it. There is no likelihood no no likelihood no no no likelihood of it.

There is no likelihood none no likelihood no likelihood of it.

What is a disappointment.

Not when it is to be very quietly admitted very quietly withdrawn very quietly.

With this and then four at a time. She Lucy might she Lucy might count count and have have to have a left to right and admittedly.

They could please it by counting it as very often it is rapidly done correctly begun rapidly done one and one two.

Very much as it is mine mine with a way to have fifteen say fifteen say fifteen higher. As ever. Sincerely yours.

Lucy Church.

Lucy Church may be may be it is Lucy Church went and went and went there. Lucy Church followed

and came and came pleasantly to have anguish. Lucy
Church came pleasantly to have anguish and gave the
impression that her mother was not up and about and
her mother would be very often there but very often
she went to see her married daughter and very often
she was occupied naturally. Of course she was occupied naturally, naturally what is the french for naturally. Naturally to be naturally naturally alike. It
is very difficult to notice changes if there has been a
war. It is very difficult to notice changes and she
says and why and it is because there is more than one
two three all out but she.

It is very difficult to notice changes when there is
very much very much very much of it it is very difficult to notice changes. It is very difficult to notice
changes.

In half and on behalf and on behalf and with and
on behalf.

Lucy Frances and whatever there has been when it
is more than if it is with them and with them with
them with them and with them to do so with them
who are with them they are without them and this is
a change. They are without them and this is this is
the change. This is the change that they are with
them. They are with them. This is the change.

He is right when he says that they do not do that
without that that that they do not do that without
that, that they do not do not do without that he is right
when he says that they do not do that without that.

How old are you and where were you born. This

might come to mean anything if more than one at a time came every week infrequently and it is very often in question. A question a question of who is who. Who can say how do you do. They can say it at the beginning and at the ending a long voyageing. How do you do. Very well I thank you.

Lucy Church is estimable and although a disappointment and although and although a disappointment there is a disappointment.

Never to separate Therese.

How do you do.

CHAPTER XLI

While waiting.

Lucy Church is going to be Edith Church.

It is very interesting if it is in time in time to be or as late. In use of it fortunately to arrange or is it with as well as well as it is very much to be had with it in the time of there being partly fortunately in arrangement and pleasure. It is might it be hers.

I am sorry you are confused.

He loved to think of sitting by the river bank to-night. He loved to think of sitting by the river bank to-night and for this purpose he did not wish to have a house bought for him on a hill but at a distance but at a considerable distance and at a considerable distance a very considerable distance which had been found in the course of conversation would overlook a stream which was a river as it is pronouncedly navigable and so it would be as well as well it would be very well very well attainably if there was no manner of doubt that they were very much given to have it return to their thought they thought about it and it was very much as much as needed that a lieutenant if he became

a captain a lieutenant if he because she an american she a very well I thank you and because of it they because of a mountain and she because of a contemporary in an interval an interval between does it do it quicker and if quicker can be heard or if it does it slower does it do it slower and can it be heard and both can it be heard or should it should it not be heard.

Lucy Church having been Lucy Church having been Elizabeth Church this could be actually her name. Could it.

Lucy Church and very much as Edith Church very much as Edith Church.

Lucy Church very much as Edith Church.

Lucy Church very much as Edith Church.

Lucy Church very much as Edith Church.

Lucy Church very much as Edith Church. Edith Church very much as Edith Church, Edith Church very much as Edith Church.

Edith Church very much as Edith Church.

Lucy Church Lucy Church very much Lucy Church very much very much very much as Lucy Church very much as Lucy Church. Lucy Church as Edith Church. Edith Church as Edith Church. Lucy Church very much very much very much as Edith Church. Edith Church Edith Church Edith Church irreligiously and so forth. Edith Church as a memento. Edith Church as a memento.

This is very great pleasure in wandering underneath trees which are so closely together that there are anemones in autumn a very few of them. They are

there and there are also great quantities and very beautiful perhaps edible but for that there need be more than there is although there will be next winter discrimination concerning them.

Edith Church how old is Edith Church.

Edith Church has been already printed as having been forty years old and so to be so it is necessary that by forty-four it is and there are only three or four years more she will be irresistibly determining to enter and leave when she will when she will may be may be may be may be to may be to may be to may be there is no hesitation after or before or in between. There is no hesitation if she says she said she said if she said do hear it in her ears.

Edith Church can be soothed.

Edith Church may be differently in reading and reading reading is there or is there not is there or is there not. This is in a way in the way of their distance a distance bread at a distance and bread and bread at a distance. Bread and bread at a distance how much is there of there and of there and of there and of there coming here.

Lucy Church in method.

It is very well to lean a back against a tree. It is very well to lean a back against a tree.

It is very well not to lean a back against a tree but to lean forward and to be knitting. It is very well to be leaning forward and to be knitting. It is very well to lean a back against a tree and everything. Everything and who are they and how do they do. Very

well I thank you. And mushrooms they have in them every element of beauty and durability of delicacy and determination and resistance and some of them are undoubtedly a great delicacy and have every reason to give every pleasure to those who find them and cultivate them. We will now go and look at them.

Lucy Church may be now not there. That depends upon whether they are through yet or not.

Why is a cover for a baby larger than for a grown person. Lucy Church knows and says it should be so.

Lucy Church is very likely to be acquainted with Josephine. It is partly that they are there that makes be very much as it was. It is very much as much so as much so as it is.

Lucy Church is very careful.

How do you do it. Lucy Church can be very vacant that is to say Lucy Church.

That is to say.

Lucy Church.

Very much included very much included in it. Very much included in it. There is very much included in it.

There is very much included in it.

Lucy Church made it.

Lucy Church.

Lucy Church has made it.

Lucy Church has made it for her.

Lucy Church has made it for her so that there can be some more advantage in its having been made for her. Lucy Church has made it for her in order that there

can be a very real advantage to her to have had it made for her.

It is a very great pleasure to hear English people say mosquito. This has nothing to do with the pleasure Lucy Church has in having made it partly made it and having finished it very nearly finished and made it for her. Lucy Church is very much as she pleased to me what she has enjoyed.

Lucy Church made no more ado about how do you do it than if there had not been in question do do they like to have them in plenty of time for Saturday. Saturday may be a place as well as a name. It may. He said so. It may.

Lucy Church away away from it. Lucy Church away from it would always be in communication because it is undoubtedly not the time to be as careful of cake as of bread. Bread and cake please plant trees. Thank you very much for asking me if I like it. Lucy Church may not be obliged to have it all may not may not be obliged to be very much more than is is in in undoubtedly as made a plaintively supplemented intentional return. It is in two in two parts. One part and two parts. It is in two parts. How do you like to have it as it needs to be more than in influence.

Influence and duty. She might be once in a while very well known as theirs altogether.

We are looking forward to it.

Lucy Church and replaces replace the sun with the sun and to-day. To-day comes two a day. How do you wish wish bone. She does not neglect a very

quick and nearly often after and before with it and for instance.

Edith Church could be a disappointment to not by sight she knew her by sight. She knew her by sight. Yes she knew her by sight.

It has been the habit to determine length by numbers. It has been the habit to determine the length by the numbers. It has been the habit to determine the length by the numbers. It is the habit to determine the length by the numbers numbers.

CHAPTER XLII

If she never sold her money this is it.

If she never sold her money. This is it. Is it. If she never sold her money is this it. She never sold her money this is it.

Lucy Church did not sell her money. Lucy Church had not sold her money. This is her money she has not sold her money this is it.

If she has not sold her money and she has not sold her money this is it.

Lucy Church is this it.

Lucy Church has not sold her money.

In this way as her as for her as for her she has not in this and this and this she has not sold it it is her money she has not sold her money yet. This is it. She has not yet sold her money nor is she going to sell her money very well this is very well this is all very well as it is a habit of the country in which she lives and where she has her present residence if she has not gone elsewhere to do something which is what she has planned to do.

Lucy Church reliably in at once there is no home in readily believe it if they are by the time every little way if there were once one thousand there and now there are three hundred there in a town. In a town. In a town to town. If in a town if in a town to town. If there were three hundred there there are three hundred there and permanently like and permanently like the y in Byrne. Who and when when is it when and when when is it with it with it can with it can can with it can James Burn can James Burn can James burn burn not with ambition but gradually not gradually but differently not differently not at all. And as much as when with and with with it with it with it it may be that any George is gentle not particularly successful not a failure and not in advantage and not partly.

Lucy Church might be might be welcome as an aid to advantage and vintage and very well I thank you and how do you do and is there any need since there are three and none of them at home. Not really.

It is very well and allowed. They decide that the mother had married the father. There are some however that have a difference between sitting here and sitting there. There are some places that have a difference between a valley and not at all. There are some places. Very well and if one if you if they if it is as much as if apples apples and not figs figs are very much much at all this year much at all this year.

Very much much at all this year.

It is very fine to think in terms of water very fine to think in terms of water in connection with how do

you do in relation to manufacture, very fine to think very fine to think in terms of water and of mother's milk very fine to think very fine to think in terms of water and in terms of mother's milk very fine to think very fine to think in terms of water very fine to think in terms of water in respect to manufacture and in mother's milk very fine to think in terms of water in respect to manufacture.

This makes it not do what is it what is it when after when after this when after there when after Lucy Church being free from care. Never having heard of from there to there.

Lucy Church made another be a brother-in-law by being the youngest of three. And Frances Frances Frances made the other be a father by being the youngest of two, and Helen Church made the mother be the mother by being the mother of two. There we are.

Lucy Church may be abandoned to her own devices but not probably. She may stay where she is but not very likely. She is more likely not to go away very far. She is most likely depending somewhat upon her inheritance to be sure to make some arrangement. She may be satisfied with what is to happen just as well as not. She is in plenty of time when she changes from young to younger from old to older from not at much to many many have it as they did. A scare crow can never be black it is not the custom of the country. A real cow can be black as nearly black as is to be found naturally naturally to be found but if it is to be found it is not more than just the subject of conversation

between Lucy Church and why is it that they are interested.

Lucy Church might be once more than ever.

One two three it is just as readily. Readily makes it be makes it be how many are there there now. Each one loves to answer in the course of conversation in the course of conversation in the course of conversation.

Lucy Church can change mushrooms to daisies and daisies to oxen and oxen to church. Lucy Church can change oxen to daisies and daisies to mushrooms and mushrooms to church. Lucy Church can change oxen to mushrooms and mushrooms to daisies and daisies to daisies and daisies to church. She is to change mushrooms to oxen and oxen to daisies. She is to.

Lucy Church she is to.

Lucy Church is to be more than more than more than not more than one in every four hundred. There are four hundred there very pleasantly. So they said in the course of conversation very pleasantly and showing both very pleasantly offered very pleasantly showing very pleasantly offered very pleasantly sitting very pleasantly once every year very pleasantly for three days very pleasantly and to be returned very pleasantly the following Sunday very pleasantly very pleasantly of course very pleasantly as well very pleasantly as well very pleasantly it is true that Lucy Church does make it better very pleasantly does make very pleasantly it better very pleasantly.

Pleasantly sounds pleasantly and which when and

whenever it does does does differ differ from from it.

That is with it with it if if if is is it is it in despair and is it is it is it in in despair of being opposite to it separated from it and being being observing of it as it as it was with with it as a screen of to be to be certain to be looking at it but it is not as far away from it from it and behind and behind behind believe and believing it to be at a distance of a river and is a river made to be in place of it established when there and disapproval. Made it made it be made it be made it be made it be made it be.   It is by and Bertha Bertha says they made it Bertha says they made it Bertha Bertha Bertha says they Bertha Bertha Bertha Bertha they they may may may Bertha may may day March and April and may may day.   Bertha Bertha march and april and may may day may day is on the day and if on the day if on the day.   If on the day.   If Bertha Bertha if Bertha if Bertha Bertha on the may may day.

Lucy Church plans yesterday as to-day. Lucy Church plans yesterday as to-day.   Lucy Church plans Lucy Church plans yesterday Lucy Church plans plans yesterday yesterday as as to-day as to day.

Lucy Church may be reasoned reasonable reason retold retold retold hold hold and held makes it in precision.   Precision makes it in in win and win win winning winning awaiting their not their return.   They do not return in return not they.

Lucy Church not they.

Lucy Church made it be left to be made it left left left he had a good place from which to see and he left

it and this did not make any difference because another place did as well would do as well. Lucy Church equably in respect to when is it that that they do like do like it as do like it do like it as when dahlias when dahlias very well selected dahlias very well, selected dahlias to to be sure to be sure to annul annul it. It might with it as in with and with investigation. Lucy Church would not would not investigate why when when is it when is it in time. They might be very plainly plainly in plainly went and came to be sure to be sure. How do you do very well I thank you.

It is not a plan this that if they go they will say so.

Lucy Church might Lucy Lucy did you see Lucy did you see what they said Lucy Lucy did you see what they said. Lucy did you see what they said, Lucy did you see what they said. Lucy did you see what they said.

Lucy Lucy did Lucy did Lucy see and see too see to it and see to it Lucy did Lucy did Lucy see to it. Did Lucy Lucy see did Lucy see to it. Did Lucy see to it.

Lucy Church and a garbled version. A Lucy Church and a garbled version. Lucy Church and a Lucy Church and a garbled version. Did Lucy Church see to it Lucy Church see Lucy Church and a garbled version see to it. Did Lucy Church with and without it see to it. Did see to it. Lucy Church did see did see to did see to it Lucy Church did see to it.

Lucy Church in adding how many trees are preferred preference and retaliation retaliation and arrive

arrive and river a river and with with and a substantial resemblance to amount to it.

Very much with it with it who is beside beside with them with them in Artemare Artemare who and where where where is it could it could it remarkably with and withstand withstand in particular actually relieve favourably as they were. How were they.

Lucy Church made no mistake in changing a woman made no mistake. Lucy Church made no mistake. Lucy Church made no mistake in changing made no mistake made no mistake as to changing redoubtably redoubtably with and believe it of her if they can that it is a very nearly a preparation of when they went and came. How did they come. How do you do. How do you do everything that is done very much as it was. Very much as it was. What is the difference between flower and flowers. He said so and he said so. What did Lucy Church mean by mentioning that it was undoubtedly not asked not because there is no asking but because once in a while inadvertently they were believed to be alike and alike as any one can know do know do know that to know that and with it with it it is prepared that alike might be when when is it when they were when they were to like it like it just as well.

Lucy Church with and without again.

Lucy Church made it in play and playful how can Lucy Church play and in playful how can Lucy Church how can Lucy Church play and in playful how can Lucy Church.

How can Lucy Church Church Church Church. How can Lucy Church how can Lucy Church how can Lucy Church Church Church Church Church. How can Lucy Church Church. How can Lucy Church. How can Lucy Church. How can Lucy Church once in a while once in a while once in a while too as to as to Lucy Church once in a while too as to as to once in a while once in a while. Lucy Church made it have it and is it is it is it and is it there now. Is she be wise be wise and to be wise and to be as wise as wise as wire and entanglement. There is no reproach to Lucy Church as there is no reproach to Lucy Church. She is Lucy Church once in a minute and every day there are thirty minutes in every way. Thirty minutes of it of it in especially especially relieving theirs as they are to have it and go. There makes no difference if she did and with it as soon as not a little not at all. How do you do intentionally with them once when there was no care for their having meant to allow it to be in time when it is by the difference in leaving it more especially with them. A pagoda is on a church and a church is in Lucy Church and Lucy Church is by the river and the river is not frozen. How do you do I forgive you everything and there is nothing to forgive. How do you do how do you do how do you do how do you do. Very well I thank you. How do you do how do you do how do you do how do you do very well I thank you.

Lucy Church made and mean I mean I mean. It does not make any difference if she is older or younger.

CHAPTER XLIII

Eight Lucy Church.

She is eight Lucy Church and very well to do very well to do. She is very well to do. And perhaps lately with it as an escape from which in particularly theirs in place and with it in accounting for and from their liberty to be able to be relieved as much within and ever ever to be as much could it be a mistake.

One two of three if three one of two with one three of two with one two of one of two and with and by and laterally as with and in and very easily and very much as it is in and coming coming and the coming coming of it in passing it to be that it is within and heard she should say so she would say that she did not in and with and add add as it is as it is with and withdrawn as well as never being able to know it as now. Never being able to know withdraw it as now. Never being able to withdraw know it withdraw it as now. Never being able to know it withdraw able withdraw it know it is as now. Now very well if they are turned leaves

which are coming back to be flower coming back to be
withdrawn withdrawn coming back to be now it is
very well welcome as the day. They knew that in
winter the days were as long were they as long they
knew that in winter the days were as long. What is
the matter with their patience with one one two and
find it to be that it is the time for family reunion and
why. Why because now now and now now it is the
time now when they leave it with it as if in to change
with if in to multiple of three. A multiple of three is
three thirty. A multiple of three thirty is after they
have left it there and which is it which is it that they
had they too they too could do could do could do they
could do what is it that if it is an object to see could
mountains in between be mountains mountains in between. How many more are there in it with it how
many more are there with it with it how many more
are there with it with it in it is a replacement of this
advantage. Come to see seasons. Possibly. Come
to see several. Possibly. Come to see with it with
them with them how can they be held to be that it is
what they did again. What they did again women
what they did again. Who knew how many Lucys
have been called Lucy Church. I do.

After it is what is made to stay. Made to stay.
Identical.

Accustomed. In place of interval and theirs is
mine how do you feel if you do not come come come
to come. And this is so and principally principally
with it with it and please. Please come and see it as

it is of interest to you and if you like it and there are
a number and there are a number will you choose one.
Will you choose which one you will choose and will you
accept it. Lucy Church acceptably and there is one
two three one two three one two three all out
but she.

CHAPTER XLIV

Usually. It is usual for after and after after a while they came to tell that they felt very well. And this was why they did more than any of them any of them is the same. Who is the same. How do you do. How do you do. Very well I thank you.

CHAPTER XLV

What happened when everybody was a witness. This and this.

They came to see her and afterwards it was not at that time but with it at all.

That was why they were in place of as if they came on purpose.

To find her and have it given to them in attending.

The difference of attending and intending. How do you do. Very well I thank you.

CHAPTER XLVI

It is about eight.

John Mary did not know Carrie Carrie Helbing. He did not know Carrie Carrie Helbing. John Mary did not know Carrie Carrie Helbing.

John Mary at a distance.

With or without it with it or without it he did not know with or without it at a distance. He did not at a distance know with it or without it. This was not only there it was there and there. John Mary and his wife Mary Mary presumably now they are married as presumably it is now winter and they are to marry in winter to prepare for the summer. They are to be married in summer as in summer they are to be married altogether. They are to be married in summer that is they are to have been married in winter and they are this winter which will come as soon as the autumn is over the autumn does not come earlier because in October it is autumn earlier and in November it is autumn earlier in November and it is autumn earlier in October.

They are married in winter so that they will be married- in summer the spring is of no importance

in the winter or in the summer nor in the autumn nor altogether.

John Mary nor altogether.

After this they were with and without with and without doubt that they would be with and without doubt there and there they would be very much occupied with it as it is of the led away to stay away to stay here. They do like what is it that on the other side what is it they went and saw one another in following in between not very high as after all it could be coming down. It is like it.

Once every once once it was once it was that it was it was when there is there as presently and diligence diligence made to repair made to repair in the middle which is when there are four there are three there and between the three in the middle there is one which is more right than between and after it after it a little while and around. This is where they went he went. Not as at all when it is at all at all likely at all at all this this in this this this is it is it is it there there it is. After it they went and went to visit where they had to have to have a rest. After a while. It is very well to have it be that it is to be reminded that apples to be reminded and crochet to be reminded and grapes to be reminded and plums to be reminded can be dried to be reminded. To be reminded.

John Mary may be twenty-two years old to-morrow which is his son.

Lucy Church who might be Lucy Church. Who might be Lucy Church. Who might be Lucy Church.

Who might be Lucy Church.

Lucy Church. Church Church Church. Readily in after it in in after in in in after after in. Lucy Church if she is another mother there is of no importance that her mother there is of no importance that her mother that her mother oxen and in oxen there is follow the leader if he calls it William William William William Albert Bigelow and after and ashamed. Who is ashamed of having caught cold. Who is. Who is ashamed of having caught cold. Who is.

Who is ashamed of having caught cold.

Add in a whistle add in a whistle whistle whistle it is not probably Humphrey. To forget to Humphrey add.

Lucy Church is one and indivisible that is to say her mother that is to say her mother very well I thank you her mother very well her mother very very well her mother very well I thank you and it remains to be around. Around water. There is hope that if there is an inundation and they are clever they will secure the fish that have been left in the around the water. It is to be hoped and they are clever that they will secure the fish that are in and around the water this water which is there in winter and in summer there is no time in summer in winter there is time in winter water there are fish in water in winter there are fish in winter in winter there are the fish there that they do find there.

This is when it is very much where when they are

there and where and where are where and when are they there.

That all depends upon one not one because a great many give orders and this is in order to be sent away. Thank them for this.

Lucy Church does and was was and was was was to be was to be away from there and who and what what is it when when is it when is it to have been helped to like this as if there is more than it and could be to be sure.   To be sure.

Lucy Church made it be very well too very well too very well too very well to do.

CHAPTER XLVII

Simon Therese face to face Simon Therese face to face to face. Simon Therese Simon Therese face to face.

Simon Therese meet Paul Paul William William. Simon Therese when he does meet him will be very much as if it mattered. Who has been very much they and dwelling dwelling upon it and so they very much with and with and with and it.

Simon Therese can be candid he can say I don't know I don't know and by this he can mean noon and alone and one and when and be in care of there and does and will and be with it and if and as and as and let and leave it to them with with should be meant in declaration of it is as well. Simon Therese in case that he went away where would he go if it was altogether so safely left back of it with in and when it is made of this which it is by the time that it is scarcely as they sent it to him. He was always just opposite to in a minute placing it in a place of where is it when left to it by the time that it is in case of it being allowed alone as much as if it could be not only as it is in choice.

He chose a blessing and made it be another with and went and very indeed can be this in time to do so.

Does Simon Therese say that if this sort of thing goes on he will throw up the whole business.

Simon Therese says it has been done by himself.

S'mon Therese may met and meant and be with it and if it is in a cloud of their being known that having left this and being in the middle there do they care to if it is wishes and delicately embroidered in yellow and pink. In yellow and pink and tall when it is wended their way to stay and be fortunately come to go.

Simon Therese had short hair and straight and black and blue eyes and a heavy body and he grew thinner. He was not attracted by their being there.

He might change from it to it.

Simon Therese in a space said he had been to say grace and he could not come.

He had been very much all of a feather. And believe him it was not that he preferred violets nor indeed wild flowers in the book nor indeed when it came to call. Simon Therese was not playful he came to I do not know why he would care to give it there to them when when with it for instance Simon Therese made it be in time be after all his be after all his. He would like to be getting it at one at a time and if if can can left left to right with with within more than if it is which is the best after it to be once in a while all as it is more place in respect to after exchange exchanged for principally mastering it by the time that partly in exchange for interested having left too having Colum-

bus in fourteen ninety two made it apparent that leaving leaving is all of it to-day to more than if inclined made it too sorely one and one and one to be thinner than very much at large as placing to be exchanged for a lake pleasure that is once at a time be in the trusting it shall after very much as Edith was alone. Edith is the name of a lake lover who can be very well pleased to have it like it too.

A lake lover. How many eggs are there in it with and when there is placed in a time that if in resting and remaining like and with alike alike to it more than if only when to be are and will make it do.

More change than surely in esteem and come and come to arresting it in front and not only an obligation but timely with by it for more than forecast when and believing very well beloving very well not to be candied so much in allowance allowing when they up and down Olga very gently to delay not the best of it in understand that having been one side broken could be red and white mended in practically in reference to in front and a ton of which when admit and why and with with can always be changed to how do you like it.

It was very much as Simon Therese can in place can can in place with and much as if how do you do to tell that it is very much as if not very much to like it the event of not protecting in reliance and with and in beside not represented as much as if when and it is and beside can it be true that when through than when through through is always made into what in left and to left and to the left to the left to the left to right right

right right he was very likely to leave it alone and was his and belonging saying and belonging belonging to meant to do. If it was expectant that it was not more than after after all how can after after once after after after all. Troubled by not losing dinner. Simon Therese is always married to Mrs. Moffat and she has taken very good care of him she is not married to him because perhaps she has another husband living and after all if he were to be sure to be go she would be very well after all as it is did he say who is a member of the family anyway. This can make Simon Therese not a mother not a not a mother this can make Simon Therese not a not a mother his mother was blonder with blue eyes and blonder and now not blonder how can any one tell from white what white is. How can any one tell from white what white is. How can any one tell from white what white is. Is it.

Simon Therese change from Simon Therese change from seriously speaking Simon Therese Simon Therese in coming complicating completing combining coming coming Simon Therese Simon Therese comes to stay and he says I do not know but she is very unpleasant particularly that is I mean that is a in between which when can call and grapes make larger in bunches which is more than pale yellow to pale yellow which means ripening that is before and behind more than is ready. It is very placidly their chant and choosing in and very much a space for an exploiting of a designing made a window and why why is it that they do not having having three as a bribe bribe makes make

it do do do for this more than at all magenta in a
blue aster become a tried of arrangement made a
carpet rising. He was so told.

Simon Therese come to see us.

Simon Therese Simon with pull and full fuller of
told and cold cold colder and gold and see seeing
saying it is settled that if in saying not this winter.

In saying that this this once two more than longer.

Simon Therese abundantly more wishes and in and
out made a day day-time.

CHAPTER XLVIII

Lucy Church was obstinate.

CHAPTER XLIX

Lucy Church how do they like their how do they like how do they like their having it.

Lucy Church how do they Lucy Church how do they like their how do they like their having it.

How do they like their how do they like their how do they like their how do they like their having it how do they like their having how do they like their having how do they like their having how do they like having their having their having how do they like their having it.

Made a way made away made away made a way with made a way made a way made a way made away made away made a way made a way made away made a way made a way made a way of made away by made away for made a way for it. Made a way for it.

Made away for it made a way made a way a way a way in a way a way to a way to a way to a way for it. Made to for it made to away made away made to away made to way made a way made a way for it.

Laid it a way for a while and so for a while to smile and so to smile with a wait and wait to state state could show a plate a plate which has been if again then with

and with put it by put it by to dry. Put it by to dry. Lucy Church is all of that she has been taught and she taught taught that taught to be taught taught ought ought taught ought to teach teach taught bought how to buy and why.

Why might it be that it is an investigate why is it that they prefer long to round and short to tall and with to that and violent to roll. Why does it make from ninety five as difined as it can be. Lucy Church is cautious.

Lucy Church was gradually coming in in back again.

Lucy Church and a pin a pin a brooch Lucy Church and a pin a pin a brooch. When it is an inheritance to inherit a pin a pin a brooch and it has been part of the time theirs to know that a mountain is Mount Blanc and that it is adequate and preliminary how many sisters has Lucy Church and how many mothers. She has one mother one father and two sisters. She is married and her husband is ascertained in respect to a rose cap upon a distant hillside which when if they come down they when they are surrounded by little pieces are very well I thank you and please be very careful of it. This may be severely and interrogatively and more often and very little when chocolate is always brown, chocolate always is. They they have two little girls the older paler and taller and the smaller stouter and fairer. And so they are. Lucy may be may be not at all happily reciprocating the question are they at the foot of the hill. No they are not at the foot of the hill at least not at the foot of the wooded hill. They are at the foot of a cultivated hill.

At the foot of a cultivated hill at some distance from a water-fall very near a very nicely covered hill and afterward behind.

What is a dead horse when there are coming and going and stopping and in a minute and everything. And seen with a house. And a square there where it is more than regularly in rows. They can wait every little while once a day in the morning. They can. It does not take long to look at last. Not at all to a nevertheless with and address it to them. It is very well to be known to be changing Lucy Church and everything Lucy Pagoda and everything Lucy Church and everything. It is very well known to be like it when it is that they recommend them to try it. And they do and very much as well as when and it is only occasional on their account that they see so that they see about it that they see to it. Always be at your very best and love to have it more than it is as they like it if if they have have stopped and have stopped and have looked.

It is by that time in and do and now not at all at any time and not any more to make more of it.

It is very much which is it when they liked to decide that it is better to name it naturally than to have it changed from Jack to Jaqueline or from Henry to Henrietta.

They like them and with it there and with beside which can as if as pleasing before it with all of it not more than as an advantage for them. They like it they say how do you do. Very well I thank you.

DATE DUE

Demco, Inc. 38-293